WINGS AND BLINDNESS
A DEATHLESS LOVE NOVEL

ZORA FOX

WELCOME TO THE EIGHT REALMS

A land of gods and goddesses—a savage, beautiful collection of islands in the Corae Sea. The stories here are violent, with explicit sexual content not intended for anyone under 18. These books about deathless love feature dark, often twisted romances. Enter at your own risk.

ZENIA

Ruled by Thenios, God-King of lightning

APHRISO

Ruled by Cytherea, goddess of pleasure

ERISET

Contested land, ruled by Ares and Bellona, god and goddess of war

MENOS

Ruled by Scira, goddess of wisdom

NALIA

Ruled by Basileus, god of the ocean

HYPERION

Ruled by Lox, god of the sun

KANTHAROS

Ruled by Vesta, goddess of hearth and home

FAR REALM

Ruled by Hades, god of the dead

Content warnings for this story of deathless love: attempted sexual assault, murder (both attempted and completed), and explicit sex including bondage scenes

❧ I ❧
PSYCHE

I sighed as I scrubbed bird droppings off Cytherea's feet. The huge statue, open to the sky, stood in the middle of her temple. Above me, the figure of the goddess held a shield almost as large as her body. The surface of the shield shone like a mirror, ideal for reflecting the sacred acts performed here for her pleasure. Now, it only reflected the violet and blue twilight.

I'd never seen the goddess in person. She lived far from my city, in a castle high on Mount Venut. Considering the state of her temple, I wasn't surprised she stayed away. Anger burned under my skin as I passed the rough cloth over the white splatters. The queen didn't deserve this treatment, either from the birds or from her subjects.

Phoebe told me once there was a time when Cytherea's temples were full of men and women offering generous gifts of food, drink, and sex. Now, it seemed the only ones who visited the temple were sailors who knew nothing of worship, but only wanted the expert companionship of the goddess's courtesans. It shouldn't have surprised me. Men had only ever disappointed me, either with their greed or menace. At best, I earned their disregard.

I pursed my lips. No one was perfect, least of all me. These thoughts helped no one. In my job, it was better to search for the best in others, lean into the pleasure of their bodies, seek to become one. I did enjoy the act of sex, and I was good at it, but it always left me a little hollow afterward. In the end, I was still alone.

Still, better safe in Cytherea's temple than vulnerable on the streets of Card. But how long could I remain if there weren't enough offerings to support the courtesans?

Visitors—even the horny sailors—had dwindled in past years. Public acts in Cytherea's temple were not cheap, and a cult had arisen that offered more affordable entertainment.

Unable to leave the temple except for a few hours at midday, I hadn't seen the cult gatherings myself, but plentiful evidence filled the streets of Card. Half the people who came into the temple these days wore enamel pins depicting white wings or else they had small black arrow tattoos on their inner thigh. It was disgraceful. Even children were being named after the demi-god.

Eros.

I scrubbed at the stained feet with renewed vigor. Cytherea was queen of our realm, not this minor god. She was beautiful and fierce beyond compare, even against the other rulers of the eight lands. She had no fear and enflamed the pleasure of her worshippers. She was everything I wanted to be, but never could, as a poor woman growing up in this dangerous city. The temple was as close as I could get.

Legends painted Eros as the epitome of male sensuality and beauty. To me, he sounded like an invented male equivalent of Cytherea. No one had seen him in my lifetime, at least. The last thing this city needed was a competing cult that drew worship from one of the female deities. Already, women struggled in this port city known for prostitution and pleasure halls. They could make a good living, but unless they snagged a job at the temple, their lives shriveled with bad treatment until they died before the age of forty. I didn't intend to go that way.

I looked up at the mirror shield. In it, a priestess with a slim silver ring hanging from between her brows poured water from the holy spring into a basin. Not everyone was willing to go behind the temple to the spring anymore. In the mountains dwelled a monster. I didn't fear the creature, but my blood grew a little chillier when people described a faceless beast, hunchbacked and wicked. I figured it might be the discarded offspring of one of the wilder gods. That wasn't unusual, but it did cause the humans living nearby some trepidation. So far, though, I hadn't heard of plagues or random attacks originating from there, except for the one. Sometimes I drew the holy water myself.

Although I was grateful for the protection of the goddess, days were slow. Too slow. Still, I'd rather be here than out in the streets, where my first seventeen years had been a chaotic mess of sheer survival.

"A gift for the goddess?" cooed Phoebe by the entrance.

I swiftly stowed away my rag and floated to join her. At the temple door stood a knot of three men—sailors, by the look of them, but younger than their tanned skin and grizzled hair would suggest. The one in the back even looked somewhat handsome. Hopefully I'd get that one.

Other courtesans materialized around me. There were eight of us in total—seven women and one man—all with gleaming, oiled skin and diaphanous white skirts. Each of us wore piercings to declare our devotion to the goddess and to ensure that we bore scars while Cytherea had no blemish. Mine was a short metal bar that ran vertically between my breasts.

The man in front, who had a hooked nose and retreating chin covered by a ruddy beard, leered openly at us.

I smiled along with the others, though I suspected it was harder for me sometimes. The man immediately disgusted me.

For a fleeting moment, his yellow teeth were in the mouth of my estranged uncle, who visited one winter when I was fourteen. My smile died, replaced with a kicking heart. My hand stretched reflexively toward the knife I no longer kept at my waist. Two years without it, and I still couldn't shake off the drowning sensation of that memory.

I drew in a slow breath, shook the straight black hair around my shoulders, and stood up tall again. This time, I focused on the man in the back. Phoebe was still negotiating a higher price with the yellow-toothed sailor, so I tiptoed forward across the stones in my bare feet to caress the neck of the man in back. The others wouldn't appreciate the gesture, but I wanted to claim him as mine. I doubted I could perform equal service to the man in front.

The clink of coins meant a dedication had been made. From the depths of the temple reflected in Cytherea's mirror, the priestess began chanting one of the traditional invocations.

Phoebe whisked away with the offering while Castor, the one male courtesan present today, poured a dabble of wine over the feet of the statue I had just finished cleaning.

I hadn't released the neck of the handsome devotee. His skin and clothes felt warm against my side. I couldn't help but notice, though, that he never looked up at the magnificent statue, but down at our mostly naked bodies. He ran a rough hand over my breast as we drew the three into a dark corner of the temple where Cytherea's mirror could see but inhibitions could be loosened.

The men didn't seem to need such prompting. We began our sacred dance, losing ourselves to the movement of our bodies. The ceiling in this corner reflected back our voices, chanting and panting.

The handsome sailor gripped me, fumbling with his trouser clasp as I undulated with him. Castor drew his head sideways to kiss him languorously on the mouth. I was grateful for the interruption. It slowed the sailor down. Erotic pleasure pleased the goddess, not only quick satisfaction. Another female courtesan pressed up against the sailor's back, pushing him against me. His eyes were hooded now. Perhaps he understood better what this experience was about. For a moment, between the two of us, he paused, reveling. Then, with a huffed breath of determination, he finished undoing his pants enough to draw out his length. It was clear he wanted me, so I obliged, hooking my leg over his hip to give him access. He thrust in, painful in his speed. Holding me in place by my ass, he knifed back and forth. I gasped and cried out and made all the noises of pleasure, but he wasn't making this an enjoyable experience. At least I could pretend in sight of the goddess.

The sailor certainly believed the lie, increasing the rhythm of his thrusts frantically. I struggled to hold onto him as he threatened already to fall apart.

Near me, one sailor was having a similar experience with Phoebe, and the other was kissing one woman while a second sucked on him. An unforgettable experience of pleasure in service to the goddess. That was what we strove to offer.

Unforgettable for the patrons, at least. A better sacrifice to the goddess would be if all parties felt the rising heat, the wet ache that built like a scream from the core outward, narrowing the moment to a pitch that catered only to mutual pleasure. But it was rarely like that. More often than not, they paid, and we sacrificed.

I tried not to be bitter. There were worse jobs in Card.

2

EROS

I groaned as I pulled off my gloves. I stacked them neatly, thumbs folded together, on the thin golden stand beside the door and covered them with a cloth embroidered with a pattern of hares.

The heavy cloak came next. I hated its deep hood, keeping me forever in darkness and limiting my vision. If it wasn't a matter of life and death, I would have burned it long ago. Light and air surrounded me as I lowered the cowl, freeing the blond hair around my shoulders. With practiced fingers, I undid the knot at my throat that held the cloak in place and let it slip, thick and slow, to the ground. In a moment I would fold it in its place on the rod against the wall, but now I needed to stretch. Packing my wings underneath the fabric all day wrenched at the muscles in my back. I undid the harness keeping my wings pinned in place.

A cool breeze blew across my skin and my groan turned into a sigh. Summertime on Aphriso was blazing hot. Even without the cloak, the sun coaxed sweat from my body. How utterly frustrating that I couldn't peel back my layers unless I was alone in my quarters. I'd chosen this room because it was the only one big enough for me to stretch my wings and not feel cramped. I flexed them now, up and out, all the way out... The movement, after my wings being so long folded and bound, hurt pleasurably. The white feathers fanned out, glorious, and I rolled my bare shoulders.

Only in the dead of winter did I bother wearing an undershirt with the cloak. All my garments needed to be hand-tailored to fit around the wings. Even without them, I wouldn't trust anyone but Olitor to sew my clothes. A common merchant could be in league with that witch trying to kill me.

Bitterness fought with relief. Even after all this time, I didn't know why she would do this to me.

The tips of my wings reached lush greenery. I fanned the leaves of the trees and plants overflowing from pots around the room. There wasn't enough light in here to make them grow well, but I had a way with living things. I could feel their pulse, their heat. Before, that never applied to plants, but my ability had only grown sharper in my isolation. I encountered so few people—mortal or immortal—that the only beings I could safely surround myself with were plants. I knew when one was dying and could tend to it. Today, they needed a little water, but were otherwise lush.

I approached the nearest one, shaking out my wings a little. I took a leaf between two fingers and rubbed the soft surface. Healthy. Infinitely better than the folds of my thick cloak.

My relief was short-lived. A knock at the door hurled me back into a foul mood.

"Speak," I demanded.

"It's Zepherin, my lord."

"What day is it?"

"The ninth day of reckoning as the moon has it."

The response proved Zepherin's identity. I unlatched the door and stood back. The soldier—ex-soldier, I reminded myself—paused at the threshold, so he could maintain the large distance between us I demanded. His height declared his status as a demi-god, but not with the regal pedigree I had. He had pale skin, like mine, and quick eyes. They flashed through worry, to resolve, to resentment in a second.

Among my servants, few knew the truth of my identity. Even now, standing with Zepherin, I felt almost self-conscious in my wings. That fact made me bite out my next words. "Why are you disturbing me?" I crossed my arms, a twinge of regret at my tone already creeping up my neck. It didn't improve my mood.

A slight twist of the lips and annoyed flush of his skin revealed the ex-soldier had to hold back his initial response for something more respectful. "The emissary you sent for has arrived."

I tensed with excitement. But hope meant heartbreak, so I tried to stuff it down. "So soon?"

"You told them to come immediately."

"Does anyone else know they're here?"

"No, my lord. Not to my knowledge. I told no one, and I had the emissary wait in the receiving room."

Air came oddly labored, as though forcing itself through a too-small aperture for breath. "I'll come to him."

"Her," Zepherin corrected.

"What?" I snapped, scooping up the cloak from the floor. My wings and back already endured piercing aches from the last time I'd put it on.

"The emissary is female."

"Tell her I'm coming," I muttered, squeezing my wings tightly closed. The result felt like a headache, except that the pain pulsed along the entire column of my back.

"Would your lordship like any help?" Zepherin raised a tentative eyebrow. Zepherin, despite his bitterness at being demoted and isolated as he tended to me, was kind at heart.

Yes. Absolutely, yes.

I wanted to confide in him. I wanted him to place the cloak and smooth it over my shoulders. I wanted to experience the warmth of a friend, if only for a moment. But I couldn't let myself trust him. My cursed heart had to be reminded every single day.

"No," I answered, trying to keep my voice even. I never allowed anyone to touch me. Even Zepherin could turn. None of my servants were allowed to stand within arm's length of me.

My gut twisted. *This damned isolation. This damned secrecy. This damned life!*

I'd settle for a flight and a fuck. The very fantasy sent syrupy longing into my bones. Once upon a time I'd had those things. The intoxication of it all set my skin ablaze even now.

I hurt. I hurt deep in my bones. Not only for all the lost nights of sex, or the beautiful time when I didn't fear. No, I mourned the death of my ultimate dream. In the midst of steamy encounters or royal parties at the castle, I always thought I'd find a great love. The anticipation of it made everything sparkle.

Now, the closest I could get was occasionally matching my servants with compatible partners. My dream, the one I'd held deep in my core, had fractured so deeply these past years that nothing could put it right. There was no great love. There was only fleeting pleasure for those lucky enough to grasp it.

I re-tied an identical knot at my throat. Would it be so terrible if Cytherea did manage to assassinate me?

I dismissed the thought at once. I, not she, would win this battle. I stared at the hares patterned into the cloth and inhaled.

"Go. Now," I ordered. "Make her ready and tell her I'm coming."

Zepherin obeyed.

I plucked the cloth off the folded gloves, put them on, and raised the deep hood over my face. Smothered. Hidden from the rest of the world again. Now, hopefully, I could free myself at last.

I STALKED THROUGH THE HALLS OF THE CASTLE, FEELING every bit the monster I was rumored to be. I had to calm down. Lox's emissary had traveled from Hyperion to assist me, or at least negotiate. I couldn't whine about my isolation or soreness in front of her, no matter how much my chest felt like a clenched fist.

Turning the corner into the meeting room, I found the obscured outline of Irena, a demi-goddess I knew long ago. A panel with intricate cutouts separated the two sides of the room so I could speak without acute fear of attack. Her silhouette was all sweeping curves, from her dark, wet hair to the scoop of her deep neckline. The tiny wooden patterns prevented me from seeing more than a suggestion of her beauty, but my skin prickled at it all the same. The castle never entertained visitors, much less someone like this.

Her heart tripped once in response to my entrance. It wasn't clear if that reaction was based in fear, surprise, or anticipation. Irena was an even-headed immortal, and I wore my disguise. It wasn't attraction. Still, that skipped beat reminded me forcefully of other situations when I'd drawn out a similar response before touching heated skin, tasting hungry lips, trailing lines of gooseflesh down to the wet and aching center...

I cursed my wandering thoughts. It had been far too long.

"Did they search you?" I asked brusquely, keeping my distance from the partition.

"Places I didn't know one could keep items," she said archly. Through the tiny holes, I thought I saw a flash of annoyance in her eye.

"Show me."

Exhaling with resignation, she drew off her dress and rotated once, pointedly. Even if she had kept some weapon or poison on her person, I probably wouldn't have seen them with my limited visibility. Besides a hint of voluptuous skin, I saw nothing. She put her dress back on.

"This does little to inspire me to cooperate with you, but

you assured us that your proposal was mutually beneficial," she said, settling herself in a seat close to the wooden divider. I hated the safety measures too, so I didn't comment. Years of endless threat had forced me to put them in place, like the walls of a cage.

I remembered Irena as a patient deity. Hopefully she'd still be willing to hear me out.

I sat opposite her. "Yes. I need assistance in dealing with Cytherea. She has been merciless in pursuing my life. These past fifty years have been hell."

"And how do you expect Hyperion to help?" She sounded skeptical.

"Two ways," I explained. "If it comes to outright combat, I'll need additional soldiers. There's no way my followers would be enough to challenge her. And ultimately..." I paused, swallowed. I hadn't even told Zepherin about this. I'd told no one. "I want full godhood. Then I couldn't die, and she would have to give up this campaign against my life."

Ascension ceremonies only took place during the eclipse, and the next one was rapidly approaching. If that window closed, I'd have to wait ten years for another opportunity.

Irena didn't speak right away. I struggled to catch her expression through the design. The scent of oil and soap wafted through and swirled under my hood. If not for this partition, I could reach out and touch her.

I shook off the thought, although it tugged seductively at my mind. In all that time—nearly fifty years—I hadn't willingly touched another live being. A dog had grazed my leg as it passed while I was walking on a mountain trail last week. Even that amount of contact reminded me of what I was missing, stabbed me with resentment against the women who prevented me from getting close to anyone.

Multiple times a year, I'd endured attempts on my life. Some of those had involved physical contact. Since I'd moved to this castle, though, the attacks had stopped. It was naïve to think Cytherea didn't know I was here. More likely, she was waiting for me to let down my guard to give her minions a chance to strike. I wouldn't give her that chance, although it grew harder and harder to resist opening up to someone, touching someone, letting someone in past the tough veneer I'd cultivated. It wasn't me. Folding gloves and barking at servants weren't me. Inside, I was weak and gullible, desperate for love I'd never feel.

"I'll have to report to Lox and ask on your behalf," she said. My attention snapped back to her.

Then, after a moment, she added, "Perhaps there's another option."

Among the deathless, Irena essentially pursued peace, but I could sense in her tone that she liked neither request I laid out before her.

"There is no other option," I said brusquely. The response didn't even sound like myself. I cleared my throat. "Irena, I consider you a friend. I know my requests are greater than usual, but so is my danger. Immortality only lasts if I am not murdered first."

"What do you give in exchange? You said this was mutually beneficial, remember?"

"What does Lord Lox need?"

She laughed humorlessly. "Nothing. Have you not considered this part of the bargain?"

All gods worked in bargains, not selfless goodwill, and they were fiercely territorial. Even the golden god Lox was still one of the Eight. Beneath his shiny surface lay a heart as mercenary as the rest. As mercenary as mine had become, I supposed. "Is undermining Cytherea not enough?"

"Not quite," Irena said delicately. She became more serious. "You know he will deny you the godhead ceremony, Eros."

I frowned, though she couldn't see me. "Why are you so sure? He's granted it before."

"Were you a god," she said slowly, "you could be a threat to him."

"How?" I tried to think. With godhood came not only true immortality but the ability to shift into the shape of other beings, a tremendously helpful thing for evading notice or attack, if Cytherea persisted.

"Eros." She spoke my name as though her absurd comment should make perfect sense. As though I were a child.

My heart beat fast and hard. My inexperience with strategy was showing again. I wanted to curse. No matter how much I considered, the only way I could think to protect myself was by boxing myself into smaller and smaller spaces. I had no head for subterfuge and deals. My friends laughed at me for it when I was a child. No matter how hard I tried, I couldn't escape the wide-eyed innocence of my natural state. "How? How would I be a threat to Lord Lox if I vowed not to oppose him?"

"There are few gods in this world. Eight have their realms. Imagine—and don't repeat my words—imagine that Cytherea were deposed and you ruled in her stead. You are a god of seduction, Eros, of beauty and passion and lust. You could lure one of the Nine to your bed and create an imbalance of power. Two realms combined into one. It's too much of a risk."

My throat constricted at the absurdity of her words. For fifty years, I hadn't shown my face. The idea that I could seduce another god felt laughable now. Would I even be able to hold a conversation?

Technically, she was right. It was that powerful reputation (and truth to support it) that drew the worshippers in the first place, like filaments to a magnet. Over time, Cytherea's temples emptied, and devotion to me grew among the human population. I'd done little to encourage that development, and yet I drew more wrath from the goddess for it than the humans did.

"Without marriage, the realms wouldn't fully merge," I protested lamely.

"Perhaps if you married someone powerless as a show of good faith," she said, rising. It was a suggestion and not a suggestion—the admission that Lox wouldn't help me otherwise.

Marry. Divine marriages lasted forever, or until the death of a partner. My heart gave a twist. Why was it so hard to give up that last shred of hope that one day I'd truly love and be loved? To accomplish what Irena was suggesting meant gathering mortal women while still protecting my identity. It was ludicrous, bordering on cruel. *But maybe,* said a small voice in my head, the foolish one that couldn't help but cling to fantasies, *maybe they will love you anyway.*

My brow knitted together almost painfully. I really was a fool if I believed that. Who could love what I'd become?

Did I choose safety or the dying chance of future love?

There would be no future if Cytherea got her way. I had to protect myself.

Perhaps I'd find a different life over time, one that didn't reek of cowardice. Maybe, maybe, I'd be lucky enough to share pleasure with my mate. Less than love—the drowning, all-consuming kind I longed for—but it was the best I could hope for.

If I had to kill my mortally injured dream to defeat Cytherea, so be it. "Would Lox help me then?"

"Try it and find out." She softened, as many did, sooner or later, even those who had tried to kill me afterward. Her temperature warmed. "I'll send word when I can."

With that promise in my ears, I could pretend I wasn't a monster, that I had friends and consorts and freedom. Closeness with someone. I wanted her to stay, even if we could only talk like this, though the barrier.

But she was gone.

3

PSYCHE

By the time the morning sky lightened enough to highlight the last bright stars, the only visitors to the temple had been an elderly couple who dropped a basket of roses on the front steps, a distraught woman who came to pray for the goddess's assistance in love, and two more troops of men looking for warm company. It was a poor showing.

We lived off the monetary gifts but, lately, food had been scarce. If we weren't forbidden from eating the food offerings, I certainly would have helped myself. As it was, I ate two grapes the other day and begged the goddess for leniency afterward. The deathless weren't known for their compassion, but years on the street made it difficult to resist such an easy solution to my hunger.

"I think that sailor bit me," Phoebe declared, tipping her head far back so we could see her neck.

I sat with the eight night courtesans around a rough wooden table with the night priestess, Belaria. All of us shared two bedrooms and a common area in the depths of the temple. Now that we could rest, a spread of olives and grape leaves had been prepared for us.

I inspected the smooth sweep of Phoebe's pale throat. As much as possible, besides our piercings, we were all to remain unblemished. The thought brought on a familiar surge of nerves.

Externally, I was unblemished.

My gaze shot to Belaria, who sat imperiously at the head of the table, her hair wrapped like a crown. She wore a maroon, one-shouldered gown. The rest of us, except Castor, had donned soft, lightweight dresses once our duties were done.

Belaria dedicated her life to Cytherea, as we all did, but her version of devotion meant inhuman perfection. Nothing we did was good enough for her, and probably not for the goddess either.

It was the day priestess who had plucked me from the streets after encountering me at the market the day after I turned eighteen. My beauty would please Cytherea, she'd said. At the time, I thought she was joking. She asked if I was a virgin. Sensing that the woman might give me shelter as well as a chance to serve the goddess whom I'd always admired, I lied and said yes. Perhaps it was my imagination, but even now I suspected she knew the truth. This was Cytherea's port city. There were few virgins left. Even so, she'd taken me back to the temple that very day.

I never told anyone my bigger secret. The priestesses and courtesans did not know, but the goddess might discover the truth.

The elderly couple from earlier had immigrated here from

Menos, far on the other side of the Corae Sea, where the goddess Scira reigned. Her gift was knowledge, including knowledge of past and future. I silently thanked the gods that I served Cytherea instead of the Seer Goddess. At least here I could attempt to hide my secret.

I tried to shake off my concerns.

"That happened to me last week," Kalli lamented after bringing her face practically against Phoebe's skin to inspect it. "I don't see any blood."

"I didn't say there would be blood," Phoebe replied.

"There's a slight mark," I admitted, "but I can help you cover it."

"I can do it myself." Phoebe shot me a glare as she quickly lowered her head.

We all had practice covering scrapes and bruises and blemishes. In our common area, there were creams and oils to deal with such things, worth more than the food we ate most days. I liked figuring out combinations that would help the others. Phoebe's dismissal meant she begrudged me the company of the handsome sailor. In front of the priestess, she would say nothing. But I knew. Too bad my choice hadn't been worth offending the others.

"Tomorrow I'm going into town," I said, forcing down my annoyance. As someone who grew up around the markets of Card, the task of shopping usually fell to me. At this point, I sometimes volunteered, just to feel more in control of my choices. "Do you have a list of what we need? Any more ointments?"

Belaria cut in and handed me a list of items. "Here. This is all."

I popped an olive in my mouth and rubbed the oil from my fingers before I took the parchment from her. The list was standard, and only included a small amount of dye for the collection. The goddess hadn't been offered much tonight, and that was reflected in the small amount of food Belaria requested. The next festival that required the sacrifice of bulls, when everyone in the city could eat meat and more people than usual remembered to worship the deathless, wasn't for another month.

Phoebe leaned over to see the list. "Make sure you buy perfume for my hair."

That wasn't one of the items. As a courtesan, I didn't have any personal money. All possessions were forfeit in service to the goddess. But Phoebe expected obedience anyway. I shot her a covert glare.

She merely gazed back, touched her throat lightly as though to sweep her long hair away from her neck, and turned her attention back to the food.

THE STREETS SMELLED LIKE DUST AND LEMONS. I CLUTCHED Belaria's list in one hand and a basket in the other. Most citizens moved out of my way, since I wore the telltale dress of Cytherea's temple. A few subtly came closer for a better look. I ignored them, attempting an expression of demure serenity. I'd gotten better at that expression lately, but it wasn't natural to me. If these people wanted pleasure, they could find it on the hill.

The day was hot and my palms grew sweaty. If I missed an item because the writing had worn away, the night priestess would find a way to punish me. I thrust the parchment between folds at the waist of my gown and picked up my pace.

Castor had offered to accompany me, as he did sometimes, but a worshipper specifically requested him just as I was about to leave. As one of only two male courtesans, he often got special treatment. I tried not to be jealous. He assured me that he sacrificed just as much to the goddess as we did. Castor was kind, so I forgave him, although I suspected that he kept a small stash of personal funds given to him by patrons. Those funds could have helped me buy Phoebe's perfume. Scents weren't cheap, even the more affordable infused wax. His money and good-natured company would have been welcome.

I was used to being on my own, but that didn't mean I liked it. Even the temple—goddess forgive me—felt lonely sometimes. Here on the streets, though, I became someone else, someone feral. Beneath my sacred skin lay another woman, and I feared her. If I didn't douse my senses in sensuality and hard labor for Cytherea, the other woman threatened to jump from the shadows and reveal my true identity.

Untamed, fierce, and afraid.

Cytherea, beautiful and battle-ready, deathless and self-possessed, represented everything I wanted to be.

A man accidentally jostled my basket as he passed. On the shoulder of his tunic, he wore a pin of white wings.

I scowled. That expression felt more natural.

The market was only a ten-minute walk from the temple, fifteen going back the other way since Cytherea's shrine sat atop of one of the mountain foothills. Even the market loomed high above the sea. Pavestone paths winding through town eventually reached a low wall that edged a steep incline down to the docks. People both good and unsavory sat on the wall to observe the ships coming in. A young man ate a thin piece of flatbread wrapped around vegetables and what smelled like meat sauce. My mouth watered as I passed him, walking parallel to the cliffside.

Near him, a sharp-looking man with a light beard eyed the horizon. His focus shifted momentarily to me as I went by. I felt his gaze evaluating me. He was welcome to the temple, but I had business to finish here. Trips into town meant I got less sleep than usual. I ought to make the most of them. Besides, I had to figure out how to get Phoebe's perfume without additional money.

My face hadn't returned to its serene state. As the market finally came in sight, I wrestled my expression into bland submission. No one needed to know about my inner struggles. The goddess came first. She wished for pleasure for her subjects, so I had to at least look pleasant. Knowing I belonged to her temple provided a slim measure of protection, too, which I willingly embraced.

This time of year, the market was held in the open air, in stalls shadowed under multicolored canopies. Heaps of spices and fruits, plump vegetables, oiled breads, and larded soaps enticed from every corner.

If it weren't for the hidden side of the city, I would love this place. But tucked into corners were lecherous drunks, pickpockets barely old enough to say their own names, and people who would gladly drug women for a price.

I inhaled deeply and approached the first stall. "Five scoops of figs, please," I said, pointing to the large spoon lying beside the display.

"From the temple of Cytherea, are you?" asked the man, a stringy fellow in his fifties. He started rolling fresh figs onto his spoon and ladling them into my basket.

"Yes."

"Not afraid to be close to those mountains?"

"No. The goddess protects us." The market wasn't that much farther from the mountain than we were.

The man hemmed thoughtfully. My basket grew heavier. "You heard about the man who was killed? How people disappear?"

Everyone had heard about the man who was killed. At the right angle, we could spot a tinge of his red clothes through the trees. That had been a disturbing day, but not much more disturbing than other days when crimes unfolded just out of sight in Card. Personally, I doubted the monster was responsible for the death or the disappearances. Strange beasts descended from demi-gods lived in those hills, not quite like average bears or deer. More savage-looking. Those could have killed him, although I'd never heard of any other attacks by those creatures.

I wouldn't have been surprised if the man had simply wanted to go away for a few days. Anyone wishing to disappear merely needed to traverse the mountain on foot. Maybe he took too many stimulants. It wouldn't be the first time an accidental death looked more vicious after animals got to him or thieves looted the corpse. The monster was an easy being to blame, but there was no crime in being misshapen or secretive.

The dealer and I negotiated a price; I paid and moved on.

I knew most of the merchants so my errand finished quickly. One woman selling zucchini with yellow flowers still attached asked me if I had ecstatic visions of Eros himself. I'd never had an ecstatic vision of any kind, but the woman assured me it was bound to come. In fact, she seemed to think I was holding something back from her. Next to the zucchini stood a statue of Eros as tall as my forearm. She must have paid a fortune for such a piece, each muscle gorgeously sculpted, from his calves to his pectorals. Her business didn't suffer from such an association, however, despite this city belonging to Cytherea, not Eros. Most of the zucchini was gone. Perhaps I should have chosen a different vendor myself. I cast up a quick prayer to Cytherea. I doubted she'd forgive me for such a transgression, but I'd accept if she could tolerate me.

Now came the perfume. I browsed a table with little pots of wax. The sun already tilted sideways toward evening. As soon as the first stars re-emerged, my duties at the temple would begin. If I hurried, I could nap beforehand.

But how could I hurry with no money? Again, I wished Castor were with me. He might admit to keeping a little extra for himself and offer to pay. It wasn't right, when everything belonged to Cytherea, but I hadn't been her ideal devotee before now either.

"Looking for a particular scent?" asked the man behind the counter, a pot-bellied man in his thirties who kept his hair long on top of his head but tied it back.

"I... don't know." That part hadn't crossed my mind. What would keep Phoebe happy? "I'm only looking for a little."

The merchant seemed to catch my meaning, because he pulled out a small stoppered pot from beneath the main display. "Musk," he explained. "For catching the eye." He winked at me.

I managed a smile. "How much?"

He told me.

"I see."

His eyes quickly roamed my face before he apparently found the truth. "I will accept trades as well."

A trade in Card was usually nothing I wanted to give.

"That necklace, for instance," he said, pointing.

I felt for it. I'd forgotten I was wearing it. The necklace never left my neck. It was a simple bronze disk stamped with a myrtle flower. I loved myrtle, the way it shot out like a spark, unsatisfied with mere leaves and petals. It was Cytherea's flower, but I'd owned the necklace before being recruited to the temple.

"It's not for sale."

"Is anything else?" He looked at my basket full of goods, then at my breasts.

"No." Buying perfume might not happen today. The only other thing I had to barter with was my dress, or perhaps manual labor, but there was little time before my turn as a night courtesan began. "I can return later with money."

"I give nothing on promise," he replied quickly.

I didn't blame him. In this city, I wouldn't either. "An offering, then?" It felt wrong to say it, but I was running out of options. A temple courtesan couldn't steal. At least, not if they were caught.

The man just looked at me.

"Good day," I said, turning away. I felt more eyes than his on me, and something told me I shouldn't linger. Phoebe could go without perfume for a few days. If she made my life difficult, so be it. I could handle unsavory chores or a scolding from the priestess, even "accidental" burns or banishment from meals.

If nothing else, I was a survivor.

The air shifted, cooling slightly. I needed to get back to the temple. I trod swiftly, but the sound of footsteps matching mine followed all the way out of the market.

Someone going to the temple, hopefully. But I was a skeptic as much as I was a believer. I cast a furtive look behind me and saw the man with the beard who had been sitting on the wall, along with another man who appeared to be with him. The bearded man met my eyes with wolfish attention when I half-turned.

My pulse picked up speed. Only ten more minutes to the temple, but between here and there lay a stretch of little-used road. I looked down at my basket. There was little to use as a weapon if the need arose.

Before I got any farther away from the inhabited market, I had to confront them. Even witnesses weren't sure protection against an attack, but my odds were better there, so I turned fully. My face felt numb with fear, but I'd schooled my expression to calm. "Are you heading to the temple as well?" I asked.

"Yes," said the bearded one. His companion smiled.

"Good." The word came out more breathless than I'd

intended. "I must hurry because they're expecting me." I raised the basket as proof.

"Of course. We'll accompany you."

No reasonable protest presented itself except for that clawing sense of danger. I nodded once, vaguely, and walked as fast as I could up the road without running. Even the men with their long legs had to stride quickly to keep up.

When I reached the temple door, I was completely out of breath. The two men, undeterred, had followed me the whole way.

"Give this to the night priestess," I said to the first person I saw.

Compared to the open road, the temple felt like true sanctuary. Here, the men could pay, experience their pleasure, and move on.

But they smiled and made excuses when I asked for an offering. The uneasy feeling didn't leave my gut, so I retreated to the room I shared with the others on night duty. The men's eyes followed my every step until I slipped out of sight.

TUCKED IN BED, I ROLLED OVER TO FACE KALLI IN THE COT next to mine. The men from the market had set my blood racing with apprehension and now I couldn't fall asleep. Even the other courtesans felt sinister in the dark. Daylight leaked through cracks between the roof and the ceiling, but the room was stone, so it stayed dark enough while we slept. Frankly, I was glad to be able to make out the shapes of the others. Their presence was often a comfort, but today reminded me too much of my past.

Sometimes I felt younger than my twenty years, as isolated as a lost child. Which I literally was for a long time. I might give up even this position in the temple if I could find someone who truly understood me and could hold me together as I slept. I'd had dreams—embarrassing in the morning—of Cytherea herself looking into my eyes, telling me what to do with my life, and holding me close in a mothering embrace.

Longing hit me with extraordinary force, a grief for something I couldn't name but knew I didn't have.

"Kalli, are you awake?" I whispered.

"What is it, Psyche?" Kalli was the sweetest among us, but I heard the slightest edge of impatience.

"What is one thing you want to do before you die?"

"Before I die?"

"This is morbid," Phoebe said from the other end of the room.

"Yes," I pressed. "If you could do anything."

"I don't know." The outline of Kalli shifted as she rolled to face me. I saw the wetness of her eyes, but not their detail. A sense of the monstrous lurking beneath the surface struck me again. Even temple courtesans had evil waiting beneath their skin.

"You'd just stay here forever." If I kept speaking and she responded with her soft, prosaic voice, my mind wouldn't conjure a creature in place of her. She would simply be a girl—real, present, mundane.

"Not forever!" After ten to fifteen years, courtesans were

supposed to be granted a wonderful place across the mountains nearer to the goddess herself where we could live out the rest of our days in peace.

"All right, not forever," I conceded.

"What about you?" Kalli folded an arm sweetly under her head, no longer resentful that I'd interrupted her rest. "What would you do, if you could?"

I knitted my brows in the dark. I'd do so many things, but I had no idea where to begin.

"I need more water," Phoebe announced. "Psyche, would you?"

When I'd returned from the market without the perfume, she refused to acknowledge me until we were out of the main area of the temple, obviously concocting revenge. If water was all she required to forgive me, it was a small price to pay, even if I had to go outside to the spring that overlooked the mountain. My charitable thoughts toward the monster earlier had soured in the dark.

"You don't have to go," Kalli said.

"It's a lovely night," I said, rising and looking pointedly at Phoebe, though she probably couldn't see me. "It will be refreshing."

Kalli made a little noise. "Be careful! Remember the body last month?"

How could I forget? It was all anyone talked about for days. A man's body, tall enough to be one of the deathless, lay sprawled in the gap between the temple hill and the mountain. He had one thick puncture wound in his heart and another in his eye. Soldiers speculated about the weapon that could have been used, while city folk surmised that the wounds came from claws or stingers. I never saw the body up close, so I didn't know. Perhaps it was a giant tooth that made the marks, but given how dangerous the city was, my guess was nothing so outrageous. If I still gambled, my bet would be on a knife.

Their fear struck me as a little silly. Yes, the creature in the mountains was dangerous, but why would it hurt us if we didn't threaten it?

Only one other courtesan besides me had been plucked from the streets. All the rest had been groomed from wealthy families to curry favor with the goddess. They didn't know what true danger was.

"I'll be right back," I said, padding out of the room.

The priestess was performing a blessing at the other end of the temple and wouldn't be finished for several minutes. She usually drew the spring water. Although no one talked about it, the prevailing belief was that she had increased protection from Cytherea, so she had nothing to fear from the monster in the mountains, whose castle overlooked the back of the temple.

Grabbing the pitcher from the edge of the raised water basin, I headed toward the back entrance, past pillars and onto the pavestone patio. In the center of the patio, the sacred spring bubbled.

The view from here made my breath catch. Green mountains towered in majestic layers until they blended with the early morning fog. The sun hadn't yet crested the horizon, but the black of the night sky had lightened to gem-hard blue. With all this grandeur surging up around me, I almost felt like I could fly.

Perhaps this was true pleasure too. I drew in some of the

delicious air, cool on my oiled skin, and turned back to the spring.

Something large collided with my back, nearly knocking me to the ground. I opened my mouth to scream, but a large hand stifled the sound, stifled my breathing. Another arm tightened its grip around my bare waist.

Was this the monster?

I bit down hard on the flesh in front of my mouth, but couldn't get much purchase. A hissed curse responded. It was a male voice. The hand shifted. At least I could breathe again.

Another figure emerged from below the crest of the hill. I'd been looking up, not down; otherwise, I would have seen them.

My heart beat a frantic, irregular rhythm as I struggled to move, struggled to think.

The men. I'd seen them before. They were the ones who had followed me from the market.

I kicked out at the second man as savagely as I could, but I was barefoot and he dodged. Before I could gather enough force to try again, he had gripped my ankles. Vertigo seized me for a moment as I left the ground. The first man, bleeding hand so firmly over my mouth I couldn't open it, held my upper body. The second held my legs. Together, they wrestled me down the embankment, out of sight of the temple.

My attempts to scream went unheard. I twisted hard in their grip. My oiled skin finally made it too difficult for them to hold on. The ground thudded up to meet my head. I grunted and got out half a call before he suffocated me again. My feet were still in the air. I was open, bare, wearing nothing but the thin white skirt.

I knew what they would do.

Did they plan to kill me afterwards?

A rumbling, primordial *no* resounded inside me. I wouldn't accept this happening to me.

My arms flew up, one still miraculously holding the metal pitcher. The first man's face had to be close to mine. His hand held my mouth closed. A clang proved I'd hit something solid. I struck again.

The men said something to each other.

I was too desperate to hear. I was survival.

My feet slipped from the second man's grasp. He didn't hesitate to grab me around the waist to pull me from his friend. I brought the pitcher down on his head next. His fingernails bit into my back, scratching as he struggled to hold on.

But now I knew I had a chance. Panting, I stood suddenly, surprising the one holding me. With a scream, I jammed the spout of the pitcher into the man's eye. I was glad for the darkness. The meaty crunch and spurt of blood rolled my stomach, but I kept on.

He let me go, clawing at his broken and empty eye socket.

Rocks littered the space near our feet—seeing them made me acknowledge a pain I hadn't felt while falling. I picked up the largest one I could maneuver with one hand and crushed it against the man's head.

He fell, impotently reaching for me, but he couldn't see and pain disoriented him. He was like a snake striking. I smashed his hand with the rock.

Dimly, I realized the other man had fled.

Hot with rage and desperation, I straddled his writhing body and kept beating his head. The pitcher fell, forgotten.

"Psyche!" a woman screamed.

I matched her tone with another strike, but the mist before my eyes was clearing. The man wasn't moving. His head was a tangled mass of blood.

The rock fell from my fingers and rolled. I tripped as I stood on shaky legs. Streaks of blood ran down my chest and arms. My lungs and muscles spasmed, cold and confused, as I tried to focus on the ridge above.

The priestess Belaria stood at the edge of the patio looking down at me. Her eyes were wide as a demon's.

"What have you done?"

EROS

The first time Cytherea tried to kill me, she poisoned my drink. The honey in it acted as a paralytic. I awoke that night unable to move. If a healer hadn't slept beside me that night and realized my distress, I might have died.

The second time was an arrow strike as I flew, but I was the better archer. By then, I understood the depth of her hatred.

The third time, she used my friend Pothos against me.

There were many other times, but I stopped keeping track of their number after Pothos. He was a member of my court, made the most delicious soups, and had the voice of an angel. I often asked to hear him sing. One night, in a drunken haze, he admitted to loving me.

I've never been known for rational decisions, so we spent a torrid night together. At the time, I saw no harm in indulging his fantasies. But, I suspect that, when I didn't continue to show interest in him, he turned to Cytherea to find an outlet for his bitter longing.

Our relationship was complicated, but I never thought he'd try to kill me. I trusted him.

That wasn't the last time Cytherea managed to reach inside my inner circle for murderers. I barely trusted myself at this point. The goddess made it clear that everyone had a price. Unless I did something to stop it, she would have her revenge.

Alone in my room, I took off the damned cloak again.

A show of good faith, Irena had called it. I'd never thought of marrying, exactly, but if that would prompt Lord Lox to help me...

I ran a hand over my smooth chin. There were so many problems with that idea. Something tugged behind my breastbone that felt a little too like longing, for one. I wanted to feel skin again, to watch my touch bring the rush of blood to someone's cheeks. The glaze of eyes, the pebbling of flesh, the cry as I gave them release.

My stomach tightened at the thought. But marriage was more than consummation. It meant letting someone close enough to harm me. That couldn't be. Although I hadn't suffered an attack in a few years, this would provide the perfect opportunity for that witch to strike. I couldn't let her.

Even if I fetched candidates from the city—human candidates—I would have to ensure they never got close to me.

I groaned. All this control would break me. I wanted chaos. I wanted freedom. I wanted the sweet companionship of bodies without wondering whether my throat would be slit.

It was the second tryst with Pothos that had almost ended in tragedy.

The marital candidates would have to be vetted extensively. I needed to choose several to make sure there was one, at least, who wasn't an emissary of Cytherea. One who would agree to marry me when I asked.

I blinked and cocked my head down. The citizens didn't know my true identity. What if they thought they were wedding a monster? Such things were possible. In other lands, and even in this one, in the distant past, women had been sacrificed to monsters to appease their wrath. If my bride never saw my face, then I could assure whoever I chose that I was a kindly monster, but certainly not Eros, demi-god of seduction, enflamer of the city's cult and rival of Cytherea.

That could work.

I called for Zepherin and ordered him to make ready a space for my potential mates. He left to prepare the back turret area to house them.

Human women—they had to be women, for marriage among the deathless had to include the possibility of children —here in this castle...

Reflexively stretching my feathered wings, I observed my room carved of mountain rock, whether by magic or monster was unclear. The ceiling came to a vaulted peak that ran the length of the room. There were no windows, only air vents, which necessitated a rotation of the profusion of plants to gather sun outside before being brought back in. A large bed layered with soft blankets sat against one wall. The meager belongings I'd brought with me were piled and hung near the too-small fireplace on the other side of the room: some clothes, wing straps, bow and quiver.

All of it so little compared to the palace I'd come from. There, I could truly entertain multiple companions.

I had my own province in the southwest corner of the island, though I hadn't seen it in years, called Silkuoma. Before I was forced to flee, I left one of my companions in charge. At the time, I had thought I'd only be gone a few months. A few years at most.

That was twenty years ago.

Did Agafya still run the province well? I barely got any news, just the softest whispers.

Traveling through the air left a signature, so I forbade my followers to do it while we were stuck in this castle, unless I expressly ordered them to. Regularly commuting across the island would get Cytherea's attention. That was the last thing I wanted.

I never claimed to be a great leader, but I usually remembered to complete my duties. More importantly, my people liked me. Agafya, as wonderful as she was, didn't grow up knowing how the deathless ruled. I chose her simply because she was willing and she was there.

Cytherea knew I wanted to return, so I couldn't. Instead, I moved around until I found this small, abandoned castle ripped from another era. It lay just above a temple to Cytherea, of all things, but one I knew she didn't often visit. Maybe she never visited. I'd never seen her in the years I'd hidden here.

Perhaps I wouldn't have to hide much longer. Not only did I miss Silkuoma, but all the people I'd left behind. I swallowed thickly. Who could I still trust? Anyone? I doubted it.

I wrenched my mind back to my plan. The women. Marriage.

I'd never considered marriage before now. I'd enjoyed many lovers but none of them had captured my soul. Other deathless gods married primarily for strategic or political advantage, things I didn't care about. At least in the past, I thought I wouldn't marry for anything less than all-consuming love.

None of the passionate affairs in my past had pushed me to consider it. I pined, I longed, I seduced and was seduced, but I never wanted to marry.

I crossed one arm and held it over my chest to stretch the muscle. This marriage could still be good. It was likely that after all this time, hundreds of years, I would never find that mythical love. My life was an eternal chase after the imaginary.

Maybe, though, I could find peace.

At this point, I would settle for peace.

PSYCHE

Belaria glared at me with bloodshot eyes. Morning light streaked harsh lines across her cheeks.

We stood in the common area outside the bedrooms, out of sight of the temple courtyard. I shook violently, still covered in blood. My peripheral vision kept finding more in new places—my hair, my legs... I fought the urge to spit, which was forbidden on temple grounds.

The priestess was trembling too, but not from horror.

From anger.

"What have you done?" she asked again. "You killed a man on temple grounds."

"It was outside the grounds," I said through chattering teeth. "And he was going to—"

"It doesn't matter."

I blinked. My lip curled. "It doesn't *matter*?" She sounded like the people in the city after I'd tried to tell someone about my uncle. "*That's common enough. Don't act like you're the only one.*"

"You killed someone." Belaria's voice was a hiss. Outside

the room, the morning chant began. "I cannot let you stay. You've dishonored the goddess."

My insides writhed. "But I was protecting myself. Wouldn't the goddess protect herself if there were two men—"

"She is a deathless goddess and you a mere girl. We cannot have a courtesan behave as you have done."

I couldn't go back out. What future awaited me there? At least here I had the chance to earn sanctuary across the mountains after I finished my service. If the stories were true, former courtesans, most of them women, tended gardens and danced in the moonlight and entertained lovers. It sounded idyllic. It sounded safe.

Out in the streets of Card, I had no money and no protection. My attacker's cohort had fled. He wouldn't let me live after what I did to his disgusting friend.

"Please." I raised one blood-soaked hand but it was shaking so badly that I lowered it, trying to hide the level of my distress. Panic gripped my throat in a chokehold. It was a few seconds before I could manage any more words. "I'll get rid of the body. No one will know what happened. Just please let me stay. I'll do anything you say."

"No."

The syllable rang like an alarm bell, clanging and echoing through my entire body. My legs barely held me upright. "Please."

"Pack your things. You must be gone within the hour, or I will call for authorities to remove you."

Authorities. Soldiers, she meant. Mostly corrupt. They would certainly execute me for this crime, if they didn't have a little fun with me first.

I had no choice. A chance at life was better than no life at all.

Dazed and weak, I tottered back into the bedroom. No one gasped at my bloody appearance. They all slept, even Phoebe, who'd asked for water. I would miss them. Our group had a strained relationship at times, but we looked out for each other. We had the common goal of honoring Cytherea before earning our rest. And now even that fragile companionship was forever gone. Leaving the temple meant never coming back.

My only prized possession, the myrtle necklace, lay around my neck, stuck to the dip in my collarbone. I changed into my only full dress, aware I was soiling it with blood, and choked back tears as my eyes wandered to Castor, to Phoebe, to Kalli.

I slipped out into the daylight, frightfully visible. Belaria hadn't moved. She met my eyeline in a severe challenge. Setting my jaw, I forced my legs to move toward a side exit. I knew without asking that I wouldn't be allowed to leave out the front looking like this. Instead, I had to creep out as inexplicably as I'd arrived.

Would Cytherea punish me for my sacrilege? Surely, she would understand my actions. The priestesses themselves told similar stories about how she wreaked vengeance against greedy, violent men.

Even if I knew for certain that I'd be punished, I wouldn't have done anything differently. I would accept any consequence that came.

As I looked back at Belaria one last time, I lifted my chin. "I would do it again," I said, voice hard as iron.

My last glimpse of the night priestess was of her widening eyes.

I HADN'T SLEPT SINCE LEAVING YESTERDAY.

I needed to get out of Card but I didn't know where to go. Mountains rose high above the temple, which I could still see in the distance. Somewhere in those hills lay Cytherea's palace, but no one dared approach it without being summoned. I wasn't sure about the rest of the island's geography. My childhood hadn't exactly been calm enough for a great education.

Card was built on a port. Maybe I'd go to one of the other realms. Hitch a ride or something. My experience with sailors didn't inspire much confidence in that idea. Besides that, the thought of leaving Cytherea saddened me, but I'm sure she wouldn't miss one lowly street girl. Because that was what I was now. Not a temple courtesan, but a street girl in a city that devoured its women.

At least I'd done this before. Angry tears bit my eyes as I considered strapping on the thigh sheath I'd given up to serve the goddess. That knife had been my closest companion for two years. It was time to get reacquainted.

I must have doubted my good luck when the day priestess plucked me up years ago, because I'd hidden my knife in a place where I could find it again.

I pushed my hair behind my ear and pressed myself more fully into a dark corner. Sailors unloaded ships near here, hauling their goods onto carts that could carry them up the steep path to the city. I'd only take as much as I needed, no more, and then I'd retrieve the knife.

I could make far more money selling my body than pick-pocketing, but something held me back. Perhaps it was the memory of those men forcing me down the embankment, or the association I had between sex and the temple. Whatever my hesitation, it hadn't faded, so I listened to it.

Two men spoke together in accents, laughing as they passed my hiding place.

"...been to Card?"

"No, but I hear there are plenty of places to fuck."

"Don't pay for the temple unless you're picky. Go to one of the Eros-suna. What's your pleasure, eh? Some of the Eros..."

I ground my teeth, wanting to spring out and tell them off for neglecting the goddess. Did they think they could disrespect her so easily? The temple was about more than pleasure. It was to please the queen as well.

The cult of Eros had spread to other lands, apparently. Everyone needed their male to match Cytherea's power.

Males had taken everything from me. I clenched my hands in my lap, the phantom slick of blood still covering them.

Resolved, I peeked out, watching the two men amble up the path. Sea breezes mellowed the day's heat and ruffled my hair. One of the men, the shorter of the two, wore a pouch at his hip. It bulged, no doubt to show off his good fortune.

Well, I could use some good fortune.

Keeping to the shadows of the failing sun, I followed them. The furtive motion made me fifteen again. My body fell into its familiar movements as though I had never left this life.

The two sailors looked ready for a good time, all smiles and bawdy laughter, and that usually meant letting their guard down. Whether they were headed for a drink or a fuck, they'd make a mistake somewhere.

My attention flashed to the temple on the hill. If I took enough money from the men, I'd leave some food for the courtesans after I'd bought some for myself. They hadn't eaten well in weeks.

As the two crested the top of the rise to the main part of the city, I heard a scream. I shrank back, listening. A scream wasn't that unusual—it could mean nothing—but my senses were so taut that a sound like that frayed my nerves. The men didn't seem to care and kept walking, getting smaller with each step. I cursed under my breath.

Another scream joined the first. My head snapped in the direction it had come from. Then, I saw it.

People shuffled out of the way of a gigantic horse. At least, I thought it was a horse. The beast's head was as long as my arm, skeletal, with clashing teeth. It reminded me of death. Chunks of pavestone rattled away as it clattered to a halt in the square. Atop it rode a man wearing the mask of a horned skull. If there hadn't been so many people for reference, I would have thought him small since the horse-creature dwarfed him. Compared to the men and woman standing nearby, though, his height made it clear that this man was one of the deathless, or perhaps another supernatural being.

The skull-faced rider didn't speak right away, but his demeanor suggested he had a message to deliver. More people peered out for a look and began gathering around.

"The thing of the castle demands a sacrifice," the rider

announced. His voice sounded younger than I would have supposed by his horrible appearance.

Gasps met this revelation. Fearful eyes turned mountainward.

"A wife. Bring eligible, unwed women to the bluff at midnight tomorrow when the moon is dark. Eight are required. Leave them. The beast of the castle will choose among them."

The rider made no threat to follow this pronouncement, but we all heard it. The thing, the beast everyone feared but no one knew, would terrorize this town if his demands were not met.

I shivered. How horrible to be abandoned by family to sate the needs of this creature! Everyone else had been right to fear the mountain. I'd been a fool in so many ways.

"His chosen one will be treated with kindness and given as much as the thing of the mountain is able to provide, but she will not return. Any attempt to follow the potential brides or see the beast of the mountain will be met with punishment."

He paused again, slowly rotating his skull-covered head as if he were meeting each person's eye in challenge. Again, though, something in his movements made him seem young, not some hardened creature obeying a more fearsome creature's will.

Don't be stupid, Psyche. I'd been wrong about people too many times, even after everything I'd endured.

With a shout, the deathless man spurred his mount and galloped away.

All the gods had a flair for the dramatic, but this seemed

particularly unnecessary. I wasn't feeling charitable. If anything, I felt nearly murderous.

My gaze latched onto the men I'd been following. They commented loudly to one another, but I couldn't hear what they said. All for the best. What wasn't for the best was that they now walked out in the open, into the square where the being had made his fearful pronouncement. The last thing I needed was to be abducted by a frenzied crowd to be sacrificed in place of their daughters.

Or... would that be the worst thing? Maybe I could spare someone's daughter a life like mine...

I shook off the thought, although it clung stubbornly to the edges of my mind.

To continue following the men without being seen, I back-tracked down the stairs.

It wasn't long before I had a follower myself. Men were like barnacles here. His footsteps ghosted over the sound of my own, getting closer. I was still processing the news I'd heard, but now I'd have to deal with this. I touched the place where my sheath should be. Why hadn't I started by retrieving the knife? Protection and *then* money. I silently cursed myself.

"Psyche?"

I startled. "How do you know my name?" Surprise had driven out fear for a moment. When I faced the youth who'd been following me, my surprise deepened. He was beautiful and tall, with a lithe, strong body. Golden hair curled short on his head. I tried to remember those deep blue eyes, but he'd never been to the temple. I would have remembered touching that body.

"Will you come with me?"

"What?" He hadn't answered my question. And he had asked his own, not demanded.

A demure smile curved his lips. It wasn't the salacious leer of a man considering his next morsel, but the self-assured look of someone who had other business with me than carnal pleasure.

"Where?" I revised, still cautious.

We stood on the steps in the shadow of an overhanging lemon tree. He idly picked a fruit from the branch above him. "Cytherea wishes to see you."

$\maltese$ 6 $\maltese$

PSYCHE

I gripped the bronze disk of my necklace as I followed the young man up an arching set of rail-less stairs. It spanned a wide moat where white swans glided below. At the top of the stairs rose a tall white castle with a red door. It wasn't sprawling, but beautiful and imposing at once.

Cytherea's castle.

The soaring points, like knife blades, pierced the sky. My heart twisted as I noticed the symbol of myrtle stamped into a granite block beside the door, a mirror of the one I wore around my neck.

After two years of service, I would finally get to meet the goddess. A tragedy that she would have to kill me.

Getting here almost killed me already.

The beautiful youth had spirited us up the mountain in a squeezing, choking blink. One moment he held my wrist and the next I stood looking up at Cytherea's palace. My knees had almost given way. The sensation was dizzying. Even the air felt thinner here, not only because I'd just traveled like an immortal for the first time, but because we'd reached the peak of Mount Venut. Although it was difficult to look away from the frothy beauty of the castle, layers of clouds billowed below us and, far away, the sea sparkled blue. I couldn't see Card from here.

The young man turned and fixed me with an inscrutable look, partly amused and partly pitying. He pursed his smooth lips before turning to the red door and producing a key. Even the key was beautiful, a pearlescent gemstone carved into a sea wave on one side with jagged points on the other.

Would anyone believe what was happening to me? Would anyone care?

My questions didn't matter, because I foresaw no scenario where I'd be allowed to leave this place alive. Perhaps someone at the temple would wonder about me, and then my memory would fade.

Disembodied grief overtook me again. I wanted to live, to love, but I was born trapped in this life with no possibility of shedding one identity for another. Many spoke of fate. I didn't want to believe in it, but perhaps this meeting had been inevitable from the start.

The youth turned the key and opened the door. Everything moved slowly, details standing out in relief as he led me forward. Inside, it looked like a palace of ice shot through with blood-red accents. Roses and ribbons and pomegranates. I ached at the severe beauty of it all. As we moved further inside, we reached steep staircases sweeping upward. The young man—the deathless male—didn't rush or seem tired as we climbed the steps. My breathing quickened as the stairs rose and rose, the view of the lower entry growing smaller. The higher we went, the softer everything became. Even the walls were no longer made of pristine marble but something cushioned, as if I could hurl myself against them and simply bounce off. If the lower level was ice, this level was clouds or sea foam. Even the scent in the air was salt and roses and the deep musk of pleasure.

At least I got to see this once.

My guide didn't look behind him. I followed his strong back through this labyrinthine floor of marvels.

The rest that had eluded me for so long beckoned. I could lay myself down here, ensconced in white pillows, and sleep. But there was no chance of that.

Cytherea, the goddess herself, had sent for me. The knowledge wouldn't sink in. It buzzed impotently through my veins like a repeated shock, but my heart wouldn't believe it.

Finally, the young man turned a corner into a domed space, white yet dim, before a tall, thin set of massive double doors, also white and red. This had to be it. The queen's chambers. Perhaps a throne room. I tried to steady myself.

When the doors opened, the room was crowded. I blinked. At least twenty young men and women in revealing temple garb, all as tall and beautiful as the one conducting me, waited on the figure in the center.

Cytherea stood on a dais, plucking figs from a tray offered by a servant. She wore a long white dress parted in a gauzy X over her stunning body. The fabric crisscrossed at her lower stomach. Reaches of smooth skin stretched up from her navel to her neck. She wore no shoes, just like the courtesans in the temple. Her long blonde hair flowed past her breasts. On her head, she wore a crown of impossibly delicate white feathers, like the stamen of myrtle.

She turned at the sound of the doors. Even that simple movement looked powerful and sensual when she did it. The servant holding the figs followed her eyeline, and soon everyone in the room was looking at me. The hushed movement stilled.

My blood froze.

Cytherea's eyes, deep blue as the ocean, bored perilously into mine. I couldn't read anything in her expression but burning. Burning curiosity, burning anger...? I couldn't tell.

The youth who had led me here stepped aside so there was no barrier between me and the goddess herself. I struggled to breathe, to swallow. My heart and hands were confused about what to do. I wasn't myself.

"Is this Psyche?" she asked. Her voice was a heavy wave on the sea, graceful and terrifying. I could have listened to her for days without tiring.

Cytherea's divine gift was persuasion, allure. She could seduce anyone to her will. At that moment, I'd obey any command just to hear her speak again. At least, I would if I could summon the courage to move, to think, to do anything.

I felt my pulse in my throat.

"It is," the young man answered for me.

"Yes," I confirmed, rallying.

"Psyche." I'd always considered mine a harsh-sounding name, but she sucked on it as though it were as delicious as the fig she now popped in her mouth. After a moment, she said, "You used to be my courtesan."

"Yes."

"But you were attacked?"

How she knew that, I wasn't sure. "Yes."

"And you killed him?"

"Yes." My mouth scratched out the word, it was so dry.

"Hm." It wasn't a *hm* of displeasure. The tiniest spark of hope kindled inside me.

For a few agonizing seconds, she carefully chose a new fig before returning to me. This time, her ocean eyes raked me from head to foot. I felt the force of her attention as though she touched me instead of merely looking. I could hide nothing from her. If she pardoned me, it would be with full awareness of my crimes. If she executed me, it would be despite my faithful service to her. I could do nothing but wait for judgment.

"You know the thing on the mountain is looking for a wife."

The abrupt change in subject made me almost lightheaded. "I heard."

She cocked one perfect eyebrow. "I believe it might be Eros."

Eros, known for his ideal masculine form, couldn't be the hunchbacked creature people had seen on the mountain passes. I had to admit that I'd heard that rumor but had dismissed it as fiction. If Cytherea believed that, though...

"Yes?" I prompted when she didn't go on.

"Because you served me, you know what a menace he is. His cult controls all of Card."

"Yes."

"I have chosen a destiny for you, Psyche. In my name, you

will offer yourself to the creature on the mountain. If you discover it is Eros, you will kill him."

I choked at her calmly spoken words. Relief and horror warred inside me. I thought I would be sick. "He asked for eight," I said, breathless. My words held little meaning. My thoughts hadn't landed in comprehensible order yet.

"Eight potential brides. I know." She waved elegant fingers as if that detail didn't matter. "You must be chosen. When you have him alone, confirm his identity and end his life."

My mind spun. I could recognize Eros if I saw him, although we'd never met. Being chosen above seven other women, though... That part seemed just as difficult as killing him. I had little to recommend me if he got to know anything beyond physical beauty. I nearly scoffed. Eros wouldn't look deeper than that. I had a good body and knew how to use it. Maybe this could work after all...

"Do this for me," Cytherea continued in that all-consuming, hypnotic voice, "and you may claim your prize."

She paused as if she wanted me to name it now.

I swallowed. What right had I to request anything from my idol? *I want to be you.* "I would like to be rewarded as the courtesans are. To live in the Venut Valley, protected by Your Majesty." I bowed my head.

The magnitude of the order splashed over me again, and I gnawed my lip, trying to stay calm.

The goddess stepped off the dais toward me.

I held my ground, but I couldn't stop my eyes from growing round with astonishment that she would approach me.

With one finger, she lightly touched my shoulder, watching where it trailed. "You can do this for me," she said quietly.

"Yes." What else was there to say? She had offered me a way into her good graces again. I couldn't have refused if I wanted to.

"Eros has taken adoration from me. It is fitting that his life be taken by the one he adores."

Adores? Cytherea's plan was so full of assumptions that half a dozen protests almost burst from my lips.

But I couldn't argue with the goddess. Especially not now that she met my gaze again with that same burning expression as before. Now, though, I understood it. It meant hatred against Eros, and the presence of a human servant that could finally exact her vengeance.

PSYCHE

Mountain breezes teased my shoulder-length hair. The girl next to me was crying. I didn't blame her. It was one thing to be on a mission for Cytherea herself and another to be abandoned here by friends and family to appease a vague threat.

I put my arm around her shoulder, a lump in my throat. I had seen a lot of suffering, but it never made anything much easier.

"It'll be okay," I soothed. The girl hugged me sideways. I got the feeling she didn't agree. And I didn't know if I was right. Even if I accomplished my goal and ultimately killed Eros, what would happen to the others?

I released the crying girl, whose sobs had subsided to fortifying sniffles, and gazed out. From this cliff we could see the city below. There was the temple. Torches illuminated movement within, but I stood too far away to make out any details. My heart ached. The queen had made it clear—succeed in this or else.

I was glad to be able to serve her in such a tangible way... if only this weren't the only option. I despised Eros. And who knew if this creature even *was* Eros? What if it chose me out of all these eligible women and I was forced to wed a monster? My breath came short, my hand straying automatically to that spot on my thigh where my blade had been.

The goddess assured me that no weapons would be allowed near Eros, and that having one would disqualify me from being chosen. She didn't want her human servant killed, especially before having a chance to exact her revenge.

"When is he going to come?" A young woman with a fierce expression moved to stand beside me. Lithe, she stood taller than I was. She squinted into the darkness. "He calls for women and then just leaves us here? It's despicable."

I gave a dark chuckle and gestured outward. "I'd rather look at this view than be fetched by a monster." I lowered my voice to a whisper on the final word. If the women didn't suspect they were potential brides of Eros, I wouldn't correct them.

"You're right. Me too."

I looked more carefully at the person beside me. Her brown braid had ragged flyaways, but she was effortlessly beautiful. Right now, she wore a scowl that pressed her lips thin.

"Are you afraid?" I asked.

"Are you?"

"A little," I admitted. It was nice to be honest about something. I'd worn so many masks in my life that I wasn't always sure what lay underneath, but now, in this moment, I was nervous. "I'm Psyche."

"Cressida." An almost mischievous glint sparkled in her

dark eyes. "Let's stick together. I can't stand all this weeping. It's bad enough already."

A footstep sounded on the rock.

Yet another sacrifice for the monster. This time, it was a tan-skinned girl with most of her features obscured by the darkness. Light from the city allowed me to see the women on the ridge, but this person had her back to it. The golden color of her skin reminded me of people from Hyperion.

So many sacrifices. And for what?

If our captor truly were a monster, how horrific to demand the blood of eight young women. If this were Eros, how selfish of him to expect this sacrifice.

Demi-god or monster, it deserved to be slain.

In her palace, Cytherea assured me that she would provide means for the assassination. I simply had to outlast the others, get him alone, and strike.

Simply. That was hardly simple. What if he chose all of us? Images of temple worshippers rose to mind—those who reveled in the feel of all of us pressing close, touching, kissing, sucking, grinding...

My skin chilled in the mountain air. As I wrapped my arms around my middle, the newcomer hugged one of the crying girls around the shoulders. She—whatever her name—was right. There were eight of us now. We should help each other when we could. This ordeal would leave all of us scarred, if not dead.

Something stepped out of the air among us. Someone screamed.

If I hadn't traveled that way recently, the shock might have sent me stumbling back toward the cliff. It was as if emptiness had ripped itself open to admit the messenger in the skull mask, pale and glowing in the ambient light of the city. He towered over all of us. Obviously, he was deathless.

His eyes glinted from within the skull, which tilted upward so I could see both eyes through the place where the horse's nose belonged. His quick gaze traveled over our little group. I got the sense he was counting. Here were eight abandoned women and he counted us as if we were livestock, a mere business transaction. I stiffened and clenched my jaw.

"You are all resolved?" he asked, his voice softer than it had been in the square.

Bolstered by my upcoming task, I straightened my spine. "Yes," I said stoutly. A few others murmured agreement.

Cressida squeezed my hand.

"Then come with me." He held out his palm to me and Cressida, who were nearest.

I stared at the open hand. I didn't like the deathless way of traveling. But I sucked in a breath and grasped his fingers, not letting go of Cressida.

A rush of wind and darkness swept me to a place with no air where I would burst from the pressure...

Gasping, I landed on my knees. They cracked on a hard surface. Cressida panted beside me. We exchanged a look before I raised my head to see where we were.

The air smelled fresher than I would have expected. Green plants and flowers flourished everywhere, almost as if we were still outside. Dropping from unseen hooks, multicolored lanterns shone, encased in ironwork. It was... enchanting.

The view I'd had of the castle from the temple suggested it was run down, an appropriate abode for a monster. Had we even ended up in that castle? A snag of panic seized me before I could remind myself that we had to be. Cytherea suspected that the monster in the mountain and Eros were one and the same. I just hadn't anticipated such a horrible being to create such a lovely space.

Another young woman materialized next to us. I caught her hand before she could fall. She sputtered and wheezed, clutching her chest. Dark eyes wide, she surveyed the room too. Terror didn't fade from her expression. Her hair was black, like mine, but hers was longer and wavy. She was tall with a lithe, athletic body.

"Not bad, right?" I joked weakly, raising my eyebrows at the jungle around us.

She met my eyes with a pronounced crease of concern on her forehead.

I caught Cressida smile.

Another girl joined us, and another. Soon, all eight of us stood gaping at our surroundings. Even with eight women and the deathless being who'd brought us here, the room still felt spacious.

Oddly, now that the time had come to do Cytherea's bidding, to get this creature alone and kill it, I felt capable, even excited to earn back my place in her good graces. Everything seemed as if I could overcome it.

The messenger tugged off the skull mask, fluffing his brown hair and revealing a pale, handsome face. He looked younger than I would have expected, although his expression was serious, almost pained. His shapely mouth had a slight downturn. With clipped movements, he fitted the mask under his arm as someone else would do a helmet. I quirked a brow, tempted to laugh at the absurdity of it.

The young man—or rather, not young, which was more likely—drew himself up to address us.

"I will be facilitating your initiation and selection process," he said. The words sounded practiced, repeated from someone else. He held himself straight as a soldier. Maybe he preferred killing people to playing matchmaker. The idea sobered me again. "Now that you're all here, he requires you to be cleansed before continuing." He swallowed visibly and his mouth tightened. His eyes darted to each of us as though searching for something. Then, with a blink that seemed to bring him back to the task at hand, he gestured toward us. "Please, leave all your clothes in this room."

The dark-haired woman once again turned fearful eyes on me, but I was already taking my clothes off. Unlike some women of Card, I had no qualms about nudity. I spent most of the past two and a half years in a semi-clothed state for the sake of the goddess.

I missed the metal piercing on my chest that I'd removed for the sake of secrecy. Eros couldn't know that there was someone among the women conspiring to kill him. Tiny marks punctured the skin where the bar should have been.

The others disrobed as well, leaving cloth strewn like fallen leaves around our feet. We looked to the young man for instruction. For a moment, his throat worked as he watched all of us, beautiful in our own ways.

Selection process, he had said. It wouldn't have surprised me if this step of the process was about more than cleaning. The messenger certainly was taking his time examining us.

What type of body or skin did the monster prefer? The idea made me shudder.

"This way." The young man suddenly turned and strode toward a wall almost entirely covered in fresh leaves.

We followed. Hopefully we would see our clothes again. I didn't have another outfit. I couldn't afford one.

A hidden doorway opened into a large indoor pool area that reminded me of a mountain spring. Water reflections webbed the rough rock walls and ceiling. Tiles had been laid around the natural edge of the water, so our slapping feet echoed loudly as we followed. Twice our number could fit comfortably inside the pool.

"Form a line."

We did. I hastened to be first. If I was most visible, perhaps the monster would choose to meet with me alone more quickly.

Although his words were curt, the young man looked more innocent this close. After an awkward moment, he jerkily set the skull mask at his feet. So, he was nervous to be around so many nude bodies, though he hid it well.

Good. Perhaps that would make him less likely to notice the small mark left behind from my piercing.

I gave him my best smile.

He cleared his throat. "Open your mouth, please."

I did.

He hooked a finger around my bottom teeth to peer inside, then he let go and ran two hands through my hair. Was he looking for weapons? His search made me especially glad that I'd left my makeshift knife and thigh sheath behind. If every day brought this kind of scrutiny, it might be harder to kill the monster than I thought.

Completing his search, he said, "You can get in the pool."

As I slipped slowly into the water, I glanced back. He did the same to the girl behind me. I released a breath. He didn't only suspect my motives—he suspected everyone's motives. This was just the first part of the vetting process. And I passed.

The water felt surprisingly warm, almost matching my body temperature. I tilted onto my back and pushed myself away from the edge. I hardly felt anything. It was heavenly.

If Eros came in as I bathed, so much the better. I kept one eye on the door where we'd entered, hoping he would make an appearance. Who wouldn't be curious about eight naked, prospective brides?

Splashing broke me out of my reverie. I stood upright to find Cressida smirking at me. Before I could say anything, though, a girl with dirty blonde hair and gigantic blue eyes had pushed past her to talk to me.

"You know what I heard?" she whispered, swimming close enough that we touched. The swirl of water from her waving legs sucked at my feet. "I heard that the monster might be Eros."

It was a common enough theory, so I tried not to react. My heart beat faster, but hopefully the water muffled the sound. "Really?"

"I think it is." She was still speaking right into my ear as a lover might. Surprising for people who'd just met outside the temple.

My courtesan instincts leaned toward touching her, so I

took a step back instead. If the messenger was watching our interactions in the water—yes, there he was—then it wouldn't do for me to reciprocate interest in one of the brides. "Hopefully," I replied simply.

She drew me back in, her soft front flush against my side. The sensuality of this woman would make for tough competition. One of my only assets was my body, my comfort with sexuality. There had been patrons that came to the temple to see me specifically, even though my personality sometimes prickled more than the others. I wasn't a perfect courtesan, but I had full breasts and hips to make up for that.

"I gave myself up to be with him," she admitted. "I'd do anything to be with Eros, even once. That experience..." She trailed off. I felt her heartbeat quicken.

"You gave yourself up?" I said it quietly enough for the others not to hear. Most, if not all of them, hadn't gone willingly and might take this woman's forwardness as an affront to their pain. I fought not to scowl, to remain pleasant. A common struggle for me.

"Wouldn't you, if you knew it was Eros?"

I already had, but I wasn't about to tell her that. "Maybe. Why are you telling me this?"

She shrugged and released me. "You seem brave." Her gaze ticked downward. Although the water obscured our bodies, I had the feeling she was looking at mine. *Not only bravery, then.* If she hadn't been annoyingly obsessed with Eros, I'd consider returning her interest when we weren't in such plain view. Without the temple, it wasn't as easy to give sacrifices of pleasure to Cytherea.

"Thank you," I said.

"I'm Gia."

"Psyche."

"We'll keep our secret, won't we?" Her tone was undeniably flirtatious. She surged closer to me once more through the water. "If the rest don't know, they won't want to win."

That had been my theory. "Right," I agreed, leaning away.

She gave me a cheeky wink and swam over to someone else, completely at odds with the grim attitudes of the majority. Gia positively glowed with excitement.

What could be so exciting about Eros that she would happily give up her life for the chance to be with him? Inwardly, I scoffed.

Cressida approached me in the pool, arms crossed over her chest. "What did she have to say?" she asked, casting a suspicious look at Gia, who had floated to a petrified-looking group of three. I doubted that Gia would be able to make them feel better. Her claim that she'd given herself up just for a chance to be with Eros churned my stomach.

"Nothing," I said, dipping below the water to wet my hair. The bravery I'd felt moments before was already evaporating. With competition to get to Eros and stringent precautions against weapons, success would be more difficult.

With a final glance at Gia, who was hard to look away from, Cressida muttered, "I'm not excited about this so-called selection process..."

"Yes," I said, glad for the change of subject, "what do you think that means?"

"He'll choose one of us instead of keeping us all as his personal harem."

The implications fell in layers between us, like ripples in

the water. What happened to those who weren't chosen? Most of these women—Gia excluded—wouldn't be happy with a harem scenario, I guessed. But if someone wasn't chosen, could they return home? Would they be killed? Eaten by the monster, if it still was a monster and not Eros after all?

My heart felt like a block of ice in my chest. "What do monsters like?" I asked, but the lighthearted question barely sounded like my own voice.

"A maiden in distress," Cressida guessed.

"That's all of us." I scrubbed at my wet hair. *Just focus on the mission.*

"Or blood!" she said, lowering her voice.

I grimaced. "Oh gods, I hope not. How are you so calm?"

"How is *she*?" She looked at Gia again. The three girls all shied away from her audacious presence.

I met Cressida's gaze, genuinely curious now.

She sighed, giving in. "I try to make the most of every-thing. Change what can be changed. If we don't do that, is life even worth living?" When she got her hair wet, a scar in her hairline came into relief.

"Maybe not," I admitted. To some degree, I'd adopted a similar strategy to deal with my own hardships.

"My parents gave me up." She said it flatly, quietly. "I'm glad to be away from them. I just didn't want it to look like this." She quirked her mouth in a rueful smile.

I couldn't smile back. "Cressida, that's terrible. I'm sorry."

She shook her head, dismissive, though her eyes flashed when they turned back to me. No matter how much she protested, I could tell her parents' decision pierced her deeply. "What about—?"

"Finish up!" The barked order interrupted Cressida's question.

I was grateful. What story would I give for how I'd ended up here? I could hardly tell the truth.

We finished slicking ourselves off and emerged from the water one by one. The young man offered us all towels, his nerves totally hidden once again. Although he looked us over, he didn't try to touch us. I appreciated him for it. My experience with men had been... Well, in a word, poor.

"Anything you want," he said, "you just need to ask for. I'll come in every day and continue the selection process."

"Will *he* join you?" Gia piped up. She could hardly contain her excitement.

The young man cast her a dubious look, laced with suspicion.

I nearly reached out toward Gia in warning, but held myself back.

"Not at first," he said.

"What's your name?" Cressida asked, apparently emboldened by Gia's outspokenness.

"Zepherin," he answered. "Here, I'll lead you to where you're staying."

I wrapped the soft towel around myself and followed him into another adjoining room full of foliage. This one mixed the natural stone of the mountain with newer building techniques. A few doors dotted the perimeter. In the center was a group of dilapidated wooden chairs, some with cushions.

Most surprising, though, was the presence of another deathless male. He slanted a glance at us as we entered, his arms stalling in mid-air where he stood watering the plants. He was as dark as Zepherin was pale. His jaw and muscles were cut.

Everyone here was gorgeous. If the monster really was Eros and he was most beautiful of all, I honestly wouldn't mind being chosen as his mate before I had to kill him. The crux of my legs ached painfully for it. The thought was terrible, so I stored it in a dark corner of my mind. Such ideas weren't treason to Cytherea as long as I did her will. A demi-god more beautiful than the two I'd already seen... Just because the idea warmed my body didn't mean I hated Eros less.

"Your rooms are there, there, and there," Zepherin said, pointing to three doors. "Get comfortable. I'll be back tomorrow."

Cressida took my hand and rushed to the nearest door. As we swept forward, I tried to scan for exits but there weren't many. No windows. There was the door we'd just passed through and there were two more along the circumference of the space. Zepherin hadn't told us what those rooms were for. I'd find out later.

No weapons to be seen.

Gia followed us into the room. Cressida's mouth pressed into a now-familiar line.

"Isn't this place beautiful?" Gia cooed. It was nicer than my quarters in the temple, but not by much. Four beds lined the walls of the square room. It had rock walls and, facing the door, a large tapestry of dolphins leaping through sunlit water.

"It has to be. It has to be," she muttered before falling dramatically to her knees. "We can make this an Eros-suna," she said as she waved us down.

Eros-suna were the cult gatherings. When I was young,

they happened secretly to avoid the wrath of the goddess, but now they operated in full view. I refused to kneel.

Cressida chose to stay standing by me. "Why would we do that? We have enough to worry about without adding something else that could put us in danger."

"Have you ever attended?" She said it so fervently that I wished for a split second that I had. Her obsession was magnetic.

"No," I admitted.

Gia gasped. "It's the lushest, wildest thing you've done in your whole life."

I silently doubted her. Word was that in the poor sections of Card, which took up the vast majority, the Eros-suna acted as the worst of cheap brothels. More than once, before I went to the temple, men had tried to lure me into the closest suna. I had known girls who went in there, who never came out again.

"We've all just been trapped here for a monster to wed, so I'm not exactly in the mood for lush and wild," Cressida said, deadpan. "I'd rather figure out a way out of here." She cast me a look.

I'd been thinking the same thing, but I suddenly didn't want her to go. Cressida was quickly becoming my friend here, and being left alone with Gia sounded a bit overwhelming. I liked quiet.

"You can go," Gia declared. "I'm staying."

Cressida's eyebrows lowered. "You *want* to stay?"

"You heard Zephin."

"Zepherin," I corrected.

"He said we could have anything we want. I wonder if I could ask for that yummy gardener outside..."

Even with my background as a courtesan, Gia's attitude grated on me. Yes, the man outside made my nerves perk up too, but he was still an independent being. People came to the temple by choice. We served at the temple by choice. It was an offering of pleasure. Requesting to dally with random workers at the castle wasn't the same.

"I don't think so," I said. "We're supposed to be selected, remember? What if *he* hears about it and dislikes what you've done?"

She pouted, sitting back on her heels. "You're right. I'll wait." She kissed two fingers and raised them in a silent prayer, not to the queen but to Eros, I was sure.

I tried to keep the distaste from my expression.

"I went to an Eros-suna a few times," Cressida said, puckering her lips like she tasted something sour. "Someone there stole from me, so I didn't go back."

"You didn't go to a good one, then." Gia stood.

"That could happen anywhere," I said, laying a hand on Cressida's bare shoulder. In Card, theft was common. But I got the sense that the thief had stolen more than money.

"I'm going out," she replied.

In our room, there was a dresser, presumably with clothes —at least, I hoped so—but she didn't so much as look before leaving, wrapped only in the towel.

To ensure I would be chosen to spend time alone with Eros (or the monster) I had to behave. Here, I wasn't a murderer twice over. I wasn't Cytherea's temple courtesan. I wasn't a poor girl scraping an existence from unforgiving streets.

So who was I?

Everywhere I went, I had to hide who and what I was. This would be no different. I just had to get my story straight.

"You really think it's Eros?" I asked, sitting on the side of the bed.

"I really do."

"Have you heard about the body?"

"Everyone's heard about the body."

I raised my eyebrows.

"An arrow wound," she said lightly. "Eros is an archer. I'm sure he had a good reason to do it." She arched her back as if imagining being thrown by an arrow to the chest. "He can bend me backwards any day."

"What if it is a monster?"

"He isn't."

I wanted to argue. Leaving people's carcasses on the mountain and stealing worship from the goddess sounded monstrous to me. But if I couldn't convince Gia that I adored Eros, how would I convince the demi-god himself? This seemed a good enough place to start crafting my story.

"My parents are fearful people," I began. "I know about the rumor that the monster might be Eros, but my parents didn't care one way or another. They just wanted to appease his wrath, so they were willing to give me up. I'm the youngest of three daughters. The others are married, so they couldn't offer them." It wasn't hard to lace my tone with bitterness. Parts were true. "I hope it's Eros, I just... They thought it was a monster, so that's what I've always believed."

Gia gave a moan of sympathy. "We won't tell the others." Her display in front of me and Cressida didn't suggest she was good at keeping secrets. "You can tell Cressida if you like, but I don't think she'll care. Eros is in hiding. What better place to hide than this?"

I could think of a few. He could leave Aphriso for a start. "You're right," I agreed. "Could you imagine?"

"Every night. What if he takes all of us?" Obviously, the prospect pleased her.

My enthusiasm was already waning. "At once," I teased. I hope hope hoped he would get us alone, even if it was one by one to his bed.

Gia squealed and pushed me. "Ooh, you're bad."

"Eros is the god of love and lust. Who wouldn't want that?"

"You think he could handle eight?"

"Why not?"

Gia fell into a reverie and I left her to her thoughts. As I'd suspected, there were clothes in the dresser. I chose a blue dress softer than either the dress or scanty uniform of the temple. It was thin and watery against my skin, showing off the curves I planned to use to hook the demi-god. I closed my eyes for a moment to say a prayer to Cytherea. I needed her poise and, frankly, her powers of seduction if I was going to prevail over Gia and the others.

The door flung open.

"Zepherin wants us all outside," Cressida announced.

It had only been a few minutes. Had the selection process already begun? Cold rinsed down my veins at the ambiguity of our situation. Hopefully anyone who wasn't chosen would be all right.

Cressida ducked inside as we exited. Seconds later, she emerged wearing a brown silk dress

Zepherin stood in the common space, looking a little put out. One of the fearful girls still wore her towel.

"The creature of the mountain wants to see you all."

Beside me, Gia sucked in a small gasp.

"But you cannot see him." From behind his back, Zepherin produced strips of cloth that hung from his hand in a variety of colors.

I met Cressida's gaze. These precautions made sizing up the god more and more difficult.

We each took a blindfold and Zepherin helped us tie it behind our heads. I expected the knots to be tight, militant, but his movements were gentle, even apologetic. I found myself liking him more. If he disagreed with Eros and his outrageous demands, perhaps he wouldn't get in the way of my mission. Maybe he'd even help.

He arranged us in a line, one hand on the shoulder of the woman in front of us. This was ridiculous. We must have looked like toddlers playing a game. The darkness made my breath shorten not only with irritation, but gnawing fear. I was truly vulnerable like this. I tried never to be vulnerable unless by choice.

My muscles seized, memories of the two men flooding my mind, drowning me. They were wrestling me down the embankment. Where had the other one gone?

A slight push brought me back to reality. We were moving. Like sacrifices to the slaughter, we were going to meet the monster of the mountain.

EROS

I couldn't wait. As soon as Zepherin told me that the women had arrived, I had to see them. My routine was a parade of endless self-protective measures. This, at least, gave me a chance to break that stifling cycle, if only for a moment.

Eight women. Among eight, I would be able to find one who didn't have designs against me. Any other innocent victims could go home. But if I discovered that any were in league with *her*... I flexed my jaw and adjusted the knot at my neck as I arrived outside the receiving room.

Zepherin waited for me.

"So?" I asked, impatience making me curt.

"They have their blindfolds on. They're on the other side of the partition, but I can bring them closer if you like."

His tone was business-like. This marriage would be a business arrangement, essentially. But a twist of guilt churned my gut nonetheless. Did any of these women have a choice to come here? In my haste, I'd demanded a showing without explaining anything at all.

That's because they need to think you're a monster.

The thought didn't comfort me. I wouldn't take an unwilling lover. The excitement sizzling along my skin cooled. Maybe none of them would be fit to join me. The sullen disappointment I wore as often as my cloak settled around me once again. I was a fool.

"I want to speak to them," I said.

"All together?"

"Separately."

Zepherin gave a small bow, but I saw how his assignment chafed. To go from being a respected soldier to my messenger couldn't have been an easy transition for him. "I'll bring them to this side of the wall one at a time," he said.

Air refused to move in my lungs. New people. Close to me. "You've checked?"

"I'll check again."

I cursed my own cowardice, but something had happened to me that night with Pothos. The faces of friends became the masks of assassins. The hot desire I loved to sink into made me weak. It was everything essential to my being turned against me. The past fifty years I'd retreated so far into myself it was a wonder I couldn't see the inside of my own skull.

"One at a time," I said again, and waited as Zepherin disappeared to do my bidding. I sent a couple more servants to assist him in watching over the women. At the edge of my consciousness, I sensed Zepherin's pulse spike. I was around him often enough that I knew his moods. Someone I'd sent in attracted him.

The idea of setting him up with a servant he liked calmed me for a moment, a welcome distraction. Matchmaking left an aftertaste of jealousy now, but I still enjoyed figuring out who, among the few I allowed in my vicinity, couldn't keep their eyes off each other. Whose temperature rose when they locked eyes?

Then, with a deep breath and a reminder that I could let myself like these women and match with them myself, I entered the room. Longing teased the edge of every thought. *What if they love you? What if you take one to bed tonight? What if you didn't have to hide anymore?*

The barrage of yearning, welling up from my deepest parts, struck me speechless. I'd done so much to silence those voices so I could get on with *not being killed*. Yet, with this impetus, they rose again.

I tightened my gloves.

Zepherin led in a girl, holding her hands behind her back. She looked so small, with light skin tanned by the sun and shoulder-length black hair, perfectly straight. I shot Zepherin a look. He had chosen only grown women, right? When they approached, I almost laughed at myself. When I could observe her more closely, I saw she was merely human, which meant she was shorter than the deathless. Had it really been that long since I'd spoken with a mortal?

"This is Psyche," Zepherin said.

Psyche. How had I mistaken her for anything other than a full-grown woman? Despite how tiny she was, she sported generous curves I longed to take in my hands, and the dress she wore did nothing to hide her pert nipples. My insides went warm.

"Hello, Psyche."

Her heart only beat a little faster than usual, which meant she was unusually brave. "Hello," she said.

My mouth flashed a smile before I could suppress it.

Her body temperature went slightly warmer too. She swallowed. "I like your voice. You don't sound dreadful to me."

"You haven't seen me."

Her soft mouth pursed. I read annoyance in the expression, but it was gone before I could examine those lips further. "I prefer other qualities than appearance anyway," she said.

"Like what?"

"Like... being generous, kind, good in bed..."

I laughed. "You have a high opinion of someone you've never met."

"I didn't say I believed you were those things. I'm still forming my opinion, so you have the chance to show me."

Her boldness intoxicated me. If the others were like her, I'd have the devil of a time trying to decide. I took a small step closer. Any more and I would be within arm's length of her. "The blindfold hasn't made you hate me?"

"I'm sure you have a reason."

That made me pause. Did she suspect...? Despite my mistrust of everyone, her belief in me burrowed under my skin and settled there like a drug. I wanted more. "I do. And how did you come to me?"

"My parents wanted to please you."

Another twist of the knife. I hadn't thought enough about this. My chaotic side leaked out despite my best efforts to be exact. My plan was already harming innocent young women. "I'm sorry." My voice went husky. "Let the others know too, if they don't already, that anyone I don't choose may go home safely as long as they don't seek to harm me or look at my hideous form."

Zepherin appeared silently amused by that last comment. I scowled at him.

"I'll tell them," she said.

"Good. And tell them I will choose a bride within the week." So little time, but the eclipse was coming, so there was nothing I could do.

Psyche nodded, her sleek hair waving. Was that the hint of a smile on her face? My insides heated with terrible, alluring fantasies.

"Do they say I'm dreadful?" I persisted, wanting her to stay longer and needing to know how much she suspected of my true identity.

"Everyone knows you're the beast of the mountain," she answered, quiet but firm. "A demi-god."

I exhaled slowly, silently, releasing my earlier concerns. It wasn't exactly an answer, but my fears lulled anyway. Was it my status as a demi-god that interested her? "And you don't care what I look like as long as I'm generous, kind, and good in bed?" I couldn't keep the smile from my face. That last one I could manage, and I'd try with the others, though I felt rusty.

She smiled too, wide and inviting. My heart clenched. "That's right." Her words were a practiced purr.

I wanted to talk more with her, to delve into her past and her fears, her suspicions and expectations. A dangerous part of me wanted to remove the blindfold and see her reaction. But that was chaos talking.

"Maybe you'll find out," I said, a little breathless.

Behind her, Zepherin shifted. An expression of barely disguised unease creased his cheek. Strangely, gratefulness flooded my body. Zepherin was looking out for me. And he was right. I'd almost torn down my carefully constructed precautions.

Again.

My gaze drifted back to Psyche, the captivating human girl, even as I nodded. "Perhaps we'll speak again, Psyche. You may go."

I watched the silk undulate around her hips as Zepherin led her away and imagined what it would be like to take a handful of her ass and press her to me, to push myself inside her...

The fantasy brought heat blooming across my neck. I had to control myself. Whoever I chose had to accept the position as *wife*, not consort. Marriage meant more than a torrid affair. If Lox agreed to support my nomination into full godhood, marriage would be eternally binding. Unbreakable. Yes, I had to choose quickly, but I had to choose well.

Psyche said she was still forming her opinion about me. I didn't see how her conclusion could be good after the circumstances that had brought her here. Still, her poise and body had already undone something in me that I thought I'd laced up tight. Were my defenses so easily breached?

I had to rein in these seductive thoughts. I had seven more women to meet.

9

PSYCHE

The words of my brief conversation with Eros still echoed in my head the next day. We barely talked about anything, but I was sure I'd made the wrong impression. I'd begun too strong with talk of generosity and—what had I said?—being good in bed. Surely, he could sense my disgust after that from my coy evasions. They rang in my ears, rehearsed and false.

Apart from some light flirtation, Eros didn't betray any interest in me. His tone had shifted to dismissive. Some flirtation was to be expected. He was the demi-god of lust, after all.

Hopefully, I hadn't smashed my chances before I'd even begun.

I smothered a groan as I stretched upward with one hand. Gia, Cressida, and I lined up on hands and knees in the bedroom. Gia led us through a series of stretches that she said would reduce our bodies' tension.

"Very good," she said, looking at me.

I deepened the stretch. The tension in my shoulders ached

from lack of sleep. I had tried to be quiet but did nothing but roll over, get uncomfortable, roll over again, and mull over Eros's words all night.

From the moment I heard his voice, I knew it was Eros himself, not some mountain monster. That was some comfort, at least. I hadn't sacrificed myself to a beast for a fleeting chance at redemption.

Though I might have done that too for a chance go to the land given to the temple servants where I could live out my days in peace.

Strangely, something in me recoiled from that. If I could have my dream—even the idea of that felt embarrassing—I didn't want mere dormant peace, sitting in one place until I died. I wanted strength—the ability to use violence, without the necessity of it. The knowledge that I could be taken seriously and defend myself if necessary would help peace to be more... peaceful.

And, if I indulged the fantasy further, I'd like to be surrounded by others who cared about the same things I did. People who didn't judge me for who I was or what I had done, who weren't ashamed of me. One person like that would easily be worth all this trouble.

"Psyche."

Gia and Cressida were in a completely different position that I was, bent over one outstretched leg. I hurried to copy them.

"What are you thinking about?" Gia pressed.

"The same thing as you, I guess," I answered quickly. The silk of my dress rode up, skimming the underside of my thigh. "Meeting him yesterday."

I'd already asked about their encounters with him. He asked them similar questions as he did me.

"Hardly a meeting, but something," Cressida said, bending fully against her leg. I was flexible, but not that flexible. "I agree with you, Gia. I think it has to be Eros."

"Shh, shh!" Gia shushed gleefully as though there were listeners at the door, but we'd been alone all day, save for meals.

"Makes this whole thing a bit better," Cressida confessed.

It was nice to see Gia and Cressida getting along. At first, Cressida seemed dubious about Gia. I had been, as well. But Gia helped to lift my spirits, even when I didn't want them lifted, and she'd shown goodwill to both of us, despite our reservations about her. It was weird that she gave herself up for the chance to be with Eros, but she didn't seem vicious.

"That voice!" Gia exclaimed, letting her eyes roll back in her head.

I knew what she meant. The moment he'd spoken, I knew it had to be the demi-god. His voice rolled through my mind constantly too. It was sweet and smoky, mid-range, crackling with possibility. It invited sin—the kind of voice you could eat with a spoon.

"Do you think he liked you?" I asked Gia, who was clearly neck-deep in dirty reverie.

She shook herself before answering, "I don't know. I tried to hint that I knew his true identity."

"I'm not sure you should do that." The blindfolds, the bodily searches, and approaching him under guard told me he wanted no one to discover the truth. That could only be because he feared the goddess.

A savage happiness rose up in me at that. She still had the upper hand in his very castle.

"Of course I should!" Gia widened her stance so I had to scooch out of the way. Her skirt barely covered her important bits now. She met my eyes when I looked back up, her expression inviting.

"Maybe keep it a secret for now," I said, focusing on my own stretch.

Eros had told me he wouldn't harm the women, but only if they didn't see or hurt him. Did guessing his identity count as seeing? I didn't want Gia to risk it. Even though she was my most dogged competition in terms of sensuality, I'd hate to see her harmed.

"I think he liked me," Cressida said.

I turned to her in surprise. "You do? Did he say something?"

"No..." She trailed off. "But I *felt* his interest, you know?" This idea didn't make her as ecstatic as it would have made Gia. She made a sardonic face and lifted a resigned brow. For all her toughness, it wasn't hard to see the bitter pain lingering in the depths of her brown eyes.

"He makes everyone feel like that," Gia said. "He can't help it."

"I didn't feel like that," I protested.

"You didn't melt when you heard him?"

"That's not the same thing as *him* being interested in *me*."

A knock at the door made me startle.

"A meeting," Cressida said, rising quickly. "I wonder if they'll send some of us home already." She sounded excited by the prospect.

As I followed Cressida and Gia out the door, I fought to swallow but my throat rebelled. I couldn't leave now. Yes, I knew the creature of the mountain was Eros, so that was something, but I'd technically never seen him to confirm, and I had to stay longer to get him alone.

even if I could somehow isolate Eros from the others, it would be incredibly difficult to get a weapon in this place. Unless Cytherea directed a deathless one to a specific place in the palace at a time when I'd be there, even the immortal way of traveling would do little good. I'd just be caught.

Zepherin stood in the center of the common area, near the furniture. The three fearful girls didn't look as frightened as they had yesterday, though they stayed close together. I hadn't spoken much to the final two. There were more women here than just Cressida and Gia, I reminded myself, and it would be good to know them all better so I could understand Eros's preferences and, honestly, so that we could simply be there for one another. Cytherea's daughters should care for each other.

"Three of you will leave today," Zepherin said without preamble. He glanced toward our group. For a heart-stopping moment, I thought his glance was directed at me, then Cressida, but I wasn't sure. "As you know, he of the mountain will chose a bride at the end of the week, so most of you will leave soon." The muscles in his neck moved with aggravation, though I couldn't tell what he would be aggravated about. "After meeting you all yesterday, he dismisses Anneth, Daphne, and Gia. Servants will see you out."

Gia's eyes rounded and her hand flew to cover her mouth. "But—"

"A servant will see you out."

The man who had watered the plants yesterday appeared out of the air. Gia's head snapped around to look at him. Her skin went deathly pale.

The dark demi-god beckoned solemnly to the women.

The other two Eros rejected belonged to the fearful group. They began shuffling forward, clutching each other. Tears streamed down the remaining girl's face, but she looked resolute.

Gia looked like she might collapse. She took a shuffling step backward.

"Gia," I said, unsure. Her mistake of addressing Eros by his true name must have been the cause of this decision. No one wanted to be here more than she did.

"No," she tried again, but the gardener took her by the arm and forced her away. He was so much larger and stronger that she stood no chance of fighting back.

"I'm sorry."

My apology hit empty air.

Gia had already disappeared.

I felt sick. Where had they gone?

Gia had revealed that she knew Eros' true identity. The frightened women were probably safe, but Gia...?

The five women remaining stood closer together. I slung an arm over the fearful one who'd just lost both her roommates, but I couldn't offer much comfort.

I clamped my teeth shut in my mouth, frustration and fear of failure threatening to choke me. If I knew where Eros slept, I would have assassinated him tonight. Too bad I had to give up my knife.

I didn't want to wait to be chosen or dismissed into unknown consequences by this fickle demi-god. But I had to.

Something about the way Gia left tasted sour on the back of my tongue. The other women had to go home safely, and that meant leading them to believe they were being prepared to wed a monster, not Eros. And I had to make him choose me in the end.

Zepherin spoke again. "The creature of the mountain wishes to know you all better to make the right choice of bride." As usual for these announcements, his words sounded rehearsed. At least he didn't bring his horse skull today.

My irritation grew. Eros thought he could just pick one of us like fruit? As though we didn't have lives at home? And all this without even seeing him?

I realized my hands had formed fists at my sides. I forced them to relax. Even disenchanted with his post, Zepherin was sure to notice. Perhaps he reported everything he saw back to Eros. They were clearly in contact with each other, at least. I couldn't afford a tale about my anger getting back to the demi-god.

"He wishes you to know that whoever he chooses may not see his face until some time after the wedding. That includes the wedding night." He cleared his throat, squirming a fraction. "Whoever he chooses must agree to those terms."

This was how he was *getting to know us*—by demanding unreasonable terms? I checked my hands, which were tightening again. Almost every male I'd met saw intimacy the same way. Subdue, take, leave. Cytherea lamented her lack of pleasure offerings, I felt sure. That her country should house such a—

"And to... bondage," he added. To my surprise, a hot streak of red colored his cheeks and neck. Maybe Zepherin wasn't quite as mercenary as the others. At least could feel shame. "But in exchange, he of the mountain will give you anything you desire—gold, jewels..."

"Because what women wants anything else?" Cressida whispered to me.

I tried not to smirk. Honestly, though, I wanted gold and jewels. With them, I could have freedom without having to scrounge a living.

I don't belong on the streets anymore, I reminded myself. *I belong with Cytherea.*

"Would he let us visit our families?" one of the other women asked. I still hadn't learned her name. She was the tallest among us, with bronze skin and a dusting of freckles.

"I can ask him." Zepherin still hadn't recovered from his embarrassment, evidently, because he smoothed down his tunic one too many times. It already looked pressed. "I've already said that you can have anything you want here, while you're still being considered, but you've asked for very little." His eyebrows twitched downward. For some reason, I was proud of us. "Each of you must ask for one thing you would enjoy to keep as my lord's bride. You have an hour to consider."

Even though his announcements ended there, all five of us, plus Zepherin, stayed in the common room. No one wanted to be alone.

What I truly wanted was a knife, but I couldn't ask for it. This display of generosity meant nothing. It only proved that the demi-god was of deathless origin. The gods could afford to buy adoration if they wished. The thought disgusted me. The very name Eros slicked my skin like slimy oil.

I inhaled and turned to Cressida, but my friend had already marched up to Zepherin in a huff. Among the chatter of the other women around me, I couldn't hear everything she was saying. Something about *ridiculous* and *this farce* and *working for him*. My skin prickled with apprehension. Zepherin didn't lord his power over us as Eros was doing, but he was still clearly a deathless one. Cressida was a human. Unless she had a death wish, she shouldn't go around yelling at demi-gods.

Zepherin didn't back down at her accusations, but an odd expression came over his face—part defensive, part captivated. He stared as if she were a curiosity he might never witness again. No wonder. How many humans defied him like this?

At a word from him, she paused her rant, lips going thin again.

I risked getting closer. I couldn't afford to let Cressida get in trouble. She was my only friend here. My mission didn't require help, but her companionship still meant more to me than it should after only two days.

"I was thinking I'd ask for a day with... my lord," I said, sidling up to her. "What about you, Cressida?"

"Answers would be nice," she muttered under her breath, slicing a glare at Zepherin. "Perhaps a final choice, so our futures don't dangle over a cliff."

I raised my eyebrows at her impertinence, partly wanting to cheer her on and partly wanting her to never speak another disrespectful word, for her own safety.

"Answers will come in time. It's an important decision," Zepherin declared, brows knitting together.

"You don't really support what he's done here, do you?" Cressida pressed him.

I bit the inside of my lip. This was going a little far.

"He's eccentric," he conceded before something sparked in his eyes, realization that he may have said the wrong thing, "but he has valid reasons for what he's done."

"Valid reasons..." Cressida rolled her eyes.

"Maybe," I said loudly, cutting in, "he hasn't experienced love and that's why he's going about it... like this." I looked to Zepherin for confirmation.

He tipped his mouth, neither confirming nor denying.

Cressida huffed and stormed away. I watched her go, lifting a quick, silent prayer to Cytherea for her protection.

Returning my attention to Zepherin, I said, "I choose a day with him. That's what I want." Ever since I'd blurted out that answer, its fitness struck me more and more. If he granted my request, I could finish my mission more quickly. Whether I got the chance to kill this monster or figured out exactly what I needed to do to win, both would aid me in the end.

"Of everything you could have?" Zepherin sounded incredulous. "His stores are endless. Just ask—"

"What if he does simply need love?" I said, forcing sweetness and sincerity into my tone.

Eros was the god of love, but as far as I'd seen, he'd done nothing but sour it. The Eros-suna weren't known for kindness but for a cheap fuck. City folk swooned over the demi-god's image with its exaggerated musculature and great wings, but he'd done nothing to help them. He'd never visited one of the cult meetings. If he had, news would have spread all over the realm. As things got worse—pulling worship away from the queen and trading in more unsavory practices—he did nothing to stop them. He was a coward and a fool.

I schooled my expression, widening my eyes and looking up at Zepherin through my lashes. "He's been alone here, without a wife. Maybe I could help him."

My throat lunged at the words I was saying.

Zepherin's skeptical soldier's gaze turned thoughtful. He flashed a glance at Cressida's retreating form before he answered me. "I expect he'll agree to that, under certain conditions." At the thought of those conditions, whatever they might be, his eyes darkened again. His jaw hardened.

"Would you ask him?"

He gave me a curt nod, his professional posture at odds with the youthful sourness in his face.

"Thank you." I smiled at him, then strode away in the direction Cressida had gone.

I found her in our room, sitting cross-legged on the bed.

"I'm not sure how much longer I can do this," she snapped before I could greet her. She picked at her skirt, pinching it hard between two fingernails before flicking it away in disgust.

"I know," I soothed, sitting next to her. "Three people left today, so he's making choices quickly, at least."

"Gia..."

"I thought you didn't like Gia."

"I didn't like her obsession with Eros. She was smart and bold enough to have done better things with her life."

Cressida used the past tense, as though Gia were already dead. I tried to swallow down the bitterness in my throat.

"That's probably true," I said. Experience had taught me to soften my stronger responses. When a patron to the temple had taken liberties, I tried to relax, but a deep part of me, like a shard of black obsidian, wanted to lash out. That part had burst to the surface two times, ending in blood-soaked rage. To lesser degree, I'd let it slip when I snapped at the other courtesans or people on the street. No matter how hard I tried to be unflappable, I had a razor-sharp edge hiding just below the surface. Wildness that made me fear myself.

At least it could come to my aid now.

"I don't want to be here." Cressida's words came out brittle, not like a sob was brittle, but like teeth were brittle when ground together.

I put my arm around her shoulders. "Maybe you should stop attacking his messenger, though."

Her lips had all but disappeared. "Maybe."

Thick silence fell. I rested my head on her shoulder to calm her.

"What are you going to ask for?" I murmured. "We only have an hour."

"Flowers. I don't know." We looked at each other. "A ship to take me away."

"All the way past the Bridge."

"To the Stygian Sea!"

The quiet turned less tense. Her shoulders relaxed, and her eyes dropped to her lap.

"We should have the power to choose or reject *him*," she said.

"The gods..." I began.

She waved a hand. "I know."

The deathless—gods or demi-gods—commanded us

mortals. That was one reason I valued Cytherea so highly. She didn't abuse her power as some did.

"You asked for a day with him? The monster?"

"Yes." I placed my hands in my lap to still them.

She dropped her voice to a whisper. "Maybe you can reject him after you're chosen."

My heart jolted. "You think I'll get chosen?"

Cressida shrugged. "You might have a better chance if you spend so much time with him. That was a risky choice."

I met her eyes. Her fierceness now burned with concern for me. There was something of Cytherea in that burning look. "I guess I don't mind risk." I bumped her shoulder. "You obviously don't either. You were yelling at Zepherin—"

She huffed. "He wouldn't hurt a gnat. The monster of the mountain just uses him."

I frowned. Zepherin didn't strike me as violent either, but people could turn. In fact, I couldn't figure him out. One minute he looked like a handsome statue of the perfect soldier and the next the presence of beautiful women made him blush. There was some deep-seated bitterness about his assignment that frequently surfaced. So far, he had too many pieces to make a true determination. The one thing I knew for certain was that men were out for themselves and would do anything to stay in control.

"How do you know?" I challenged.

"I've yelled at him before."

I sat up. "When?"

"Yesterday. Well..." She cocked her head. "It wasn't really yelling. I just told him my opinion of what was happening."

"That probably felt like yelling to him."

She waggled her head noncommittally. "We don't have a lot of power left, you know? Days. The monster will choose a bride in just a few days. Who knows what will happen to the ones who aren't chosen? So I see this could go three ways for me." She held up a finger. "One, I get chosen." She grimaced and raised a brow. "A beautiful voice isn't every woman's dream. Two, I get... eliminated."

I opened my mouth to protest.

"And three, I am sent home. Intact." Her neck and cheeks flushed red. Even her fierce eyes turned red. "Psyche, I can't go home. I can't. Not after this."

Not after they gave her up. I didn't blame her.

No meaningful response welled up among the churning debris in my mind. What could I even wish for her?

Instead of words, I gave her solidarity. Flinging my arms around her, I held her close. She squeezed back, but I felt resolve in her touch. Cressida wasn't easy to break. She wasn't quick to cry. Whatever strength she had left, she clutched with ruthless resolve. The lines of her arms declared it.

Was there a way I could help Cressida find another ending?

When we released each other, she sniffed. "Here I am, sniveling all over myself. I'd rather be yelling at Zepherin."

I gave a watery laugh. "Yell at him as much as you want. Someone has to hear the truth."

"That this is all bullshit."

I nodded.

Cressida grew serious again. "You're brave, you know, asking to spend time with him. Do you really believe all that stuff about love that you told Z?"

"People who haven't experienced love sometimes do

terrible things without realizing how much they're hurting others," I said carefully.

"So you think the monster needs a hug?" She raised an incredulous brow.

"If the blindfolds are any indication—"

"And the bondage."

"Then he needs more than a hug."

Cressida smoothed the silk skirt of her dress. "Just be careful, Psyche. We don't even know what he is—a hunchback, a snake creature, a shifter..."

"I'll try to find out."

"And *then* you can reject him."

"Not so loud," I hissed, but I was laughing.

10

EROS

"Zepherin," I greeted huskily as he approached. He still stood far enough away that I felt safe returning my gaze to the tree I targeted below in a ravine. I squinted one eye, raised my elbow perpendicular to the bow, and released.

A bird rustled out of the branches, squawking in surprise as my arrow thunked into the wood.

"Very good," Zepherin said, like a requirement. He wasn't here to compliment me. I checked his hands for weapons.

"What is it?" I asked, dropping the new arrow I'd half-pulled out of the quiver. This damn cloak made my movements sluggish. At least archery didn't depend on speed so much as accuracy.

"The women have given me their requests." He paused at a respectful distance, both of us on a sheltered part of the mountainside invisible to the city beyond. A skeletal stallion—a non-shifting demi-god itself—grazed in a patch of grass a stone's throw from Zepherin, unperturbed by my archery practice.

My heart lurched behind my ribs. Such a simple thing, and yet I burned for news. "And you told them everything I said? About the conditions?"

"Yes, yes." His cheeks warmed. Part of me wished I could have been there to overhear Zepherin—usually much more strait-laced than my court at home—telling the women that I required bondage during sex, at least at the beginning. Once I trusted them, then I'd pleasure them however they wanted. And they would pleasure me. And I could finally touch naked skin, losing myself in sweaty ecstasy as I made her shake while I—

"Psyche asked for a meeting. With you."

My attention snapped back to Zepherin. My imagination had made me half-hard. "What?"

"That's what Psyche asked for. I said I'd check with you."

I frowned. One woman already had revealed that she knew my identity. Did Psyche know too? Was that why she wanted a meeting?

"Not alone," I clarified, fearing the depth of my own excitement. The words felt like a shield before I could say anything dangerously impulsive.

"It sounded like that's what she wants. I can just tell her that you'll give gold or—"

"No." I tugged at the neck of my cloak. It felt tight against my adam's apple. Psyche. She was the first one I'd met, the one who said she wanted to be with someone kind and generous and good in bed. The one with cheeky responses and a calm heartbeat. The one with lush, maddening curves. My impression of her had been nothing but positive. "Tell her I'll grant the request. I'll just have someone else there too. And she'll be blindfolded." I spat the final words out of necessity, but they tasted like ashes. Only my assent to her request felt honest. I could talk to her, get to know her, parts of ourselves twining together, two lives overlapping...

It would be a simple meeting, not even alone, but anything resembling intimacy, even that between friends, made my blood warm with anticipation. When Psyche and I met, I wouldn't be alone. Something loosened inside me, my muscles relaxing. Even my wings, strapped viciously under the cloak, didn't ache as badly.

"Did any of the others want that too?" I asked. The five remaining women all had allured me in different ways.

"Just her."

His answer hurt, confirming dark suspicions I couldn't verbalize. It shouldn't have hurt, but it did.

Because this isn't a normal courtship, I chided myself. It didn't matter if they got to know me. I was the monster of the mountain. I'd choose my bride, and that was it, as far as they were concerned. Psyche, though, seemed to think better of me. I had thought some of the others did too. They didn't all quaver in my presence. Some seemed interested in who I was, what personality or gifts I had.

"There are only five left," I mused. *And I only have a few days to decide.* "I'll meet with all of them. You won't have to chaperone every meeting," I hastened to add. "Olitor will help."

Olitor's job was mainly to help keep the plants alive. I was too disorganized to manage all of them. He didn't often come into my presence, but I trusted him with certain jobs, like whisking away the two most fearful girls. I couldn't stomach keeping them in the group. This union would be... fast, but mutually agreed upon, not thrust upon terrified humans who couldn't object.

Zepherin's skin heated. It was only slight rise, but I caught it. His mouth opened, then closed.

Olitor? Was he the one Zepherin had blushed for earlier?

"Or I could have both of you there," I revised. "For safety. I think that would be best."

"For safety?" he repeated, heartbeat kicking up. "Are you planning to let them near you?" My scheme was working. Olitor wasn't serious with anyone. Maybe a fling would help Zepherin relax in his new role as my assistant. They could even find love together. I nearly smiled.

I waved a hand toward him. "No, we'll just be like this. No one will get closer until I choose."

Zepherin released a breath. "Psyche will feel excluded if everyone gets the same thing *and* the gift they asked for."

I hadn't thought of that. "I'll start with Psyche, then, and you can help me figure out the best way to spend time with the others. To make it fair."

Zepherin set his jaw. A subordinate that hated the suggestion. Not a friend who wanted to help.

"Is there a problem?" I asked, my mood souring. I lifted an arrow from the quiver at my back.

"What if they don't all want to?"

"What, meet? Why wouldn't they want to talk to me?" *I might be a monster, but they haven't gotten to know me yet.*

I could tell he was chewing the inside of his lip, like a child caught lying. I narrowed my eyes. Finally, he seemed to reach a resolve. "You can't think of any reason?" he challenged.

I refused to answer the question. I could think of plenty, legitimate and illegitimate, but I thought I had gotten rid of the potential brides who were too frightened to talk to me. Maybe others were angry instead of sad to be taken away from their homes. I resisted the urge to run a hand down my face. The sooner this was over with, the better. I wasn't proud of the way I'd gathered these women, but at least a couple seemed interested in pairing with me. Being a demi-god, no matter how deformed, had perks—deathless children, for example. Surely many women wanted that.

The longer I thought about it, the more upset I grew. Hopefully someone would be willing to be my partner.

Meeting Zepherin's eye again, I saw my fears come to life. The ex-soldier I'd brought from Silkuoma didn't appreciate his lot as my personal assistant. If my servants had their way, I'd be utterly alone. As alone as a scream in the void.

My skin went cold.

"Zeph..." I began.

"I can talk to them," he said, words clipped and dismissive. Then he softened a little. Maybe he read the pain in my face. "I'll try to convince them that you're not too bad."

"Generous."

"Just following orders."

There it was again. The instant I thought I might have a

friend in Zepherin, he reminded me of our distance. That our association, for him, was punishment.

"We'll start with Psyche then," I growled, looking away from him, though I couldn't tear all my attention toward the tree where I now aimed my arrow.

When I shot, I missed.

PSYCHE

Zepherin tightened my blindfold, blocking out my view of Cressida, who was giving me a sardonic look. Maybe she didn't understand why I wanted to meet with Eros alone, but I did. If we could be in the same room, just the two of us, even if I was blindfolded, I could learn his weaknesses, his secrets. I could seduce him to choose me. Though, as Zepherin placed his hand on my shoulder to lead me out, the idea of seducing Eros sounded unpleasant. I was used to sex. Lots of it, with many different people. But this was Eros, the one who had stolen adoration from Queen Cytherea and poisoned my city with his cheap, blasphemous Eros-suna. Despite the sensual images of him I'd seen, his name didn't summon much heat to my limbs. Well, at least not the heat of lust. Of rage, sure.

I tried to summon the memory of his velvety voice and the almost obscenely gorgeous sculptures in the marketplace. I could do this. No problem. I was a professional.

The earthy smell of the women's plant-filled common room

faded away, replaced by the faint scent of vinegar. It reminded me of cleaning the temple. I wrinkled my nose before remembering to school my features.

Zepherin's grip on my shoulder tightened. Had he noticed my look of disgust?

"Is this her?" asked a voice I'd never heard before.

"Psyche," Zepherin answered.

"He said I should join you."

"I don't think we need two."

My body stiffened. Two men. Two *demi-gods*. Would this be anything like my experience in the back of the temple? If these two grabbed me, I wouldn't be able to see it coming. And if they did, would anyone help? We were outside the women's area, in another part of the building. My heart pounded painfully. Belaria the priestess hadn't helped. She'd blamed me for killing one of my attackers.

My hands balled into fists and relaxed. I forced my heart to slow. At the end of the brief meeting that had upended my life, the goddess had told me she would provide me with a weapon when the time was right.

And it wasn't Zepherin I needed to worry about. It was Eros. This meeting right now was for securing my place at his side, showing he could trust me enough to be alone with him. Lashing out at my chaperons wouldn't accomplish that.

"It's just one human," said Zepherin icily. "I think I can manage."

The reply was as immovable and slow as a shrug. "I'm just telling you what he commanded."

I sighed, reality setting in. Eros and I wouldn't be completely alone for this meeting.

So be it. I could still worm my way through his defenses while others watched. I'd certainly done it before. He would choose me. He had to.

My future depended on it. If I got sent back or killed or whatever had happened to Gia and the others, I would have nowhere to go. Cytherea would abandon me. The temple wouldn't accept me. I couldn't afford passage to anywhere, even the Bridge. I'd have no choice but to scrounge on the streets, stealing or selling my body. Unless I killed Eros, I would never be safe again.

Zepherin continued to softly rebuff the other male voice, but it was clear that he was going to join our little band.

I must have seemed awfully dangerous. My lips quirked.

"This way," Zepherin said, turning me in a different direction.

The other voice balked. "Are you sure he wants—?"

"That's what he said."

"But we can't—"

"*I* have." There was a tiny note of pride in Zepherin's tone.

"You've gone in there?"

"Haven't you, to tend the plants?"

The second voice. It had to be the handsome gardener I'd seen. I decided to picture him like that, even if I was wrong. Being blind made this entire experience more unreal, as if I were floating through a dream. Picturing the men grounded me.

A knock sounded on a hollow door.

"What day is it?" I recognized Eros' voice, this time sharp despite being in the next room.

"He doesn't allow anyone in there," the gardener protested.

My ears perked up. Eros' private space?

"The ninth day of reckoning as the moon has it," Zepherin answered loudly. Then, quieter, "This is where he said to meet, so either leave or get in."

Hesitation, then a door creaked. Zepherin urged me forward. Footsteps followed. I'd have a full audience.

Now the vinegar smell dissolved into something else. There were plants in here, wet and alive, along with something musky and slightly sweet. The effect was comfortable and sharp-edged at once, pulling me down into reveries of losing myself in pleasure. Warm, urgent, aching—like the anticipation of a first torrid kiss. How long since I had thought of that first one? Now, even sex didn't usually arouse me like that first kiss did. I wanted to feel that hum again, that pulsing heartbeat, the need to be close, to surge against each other after thick longing.

"Psyche." Eros' level voice pulled me out of my daydreams. I felt heavy with them. What was wrong with me?

I didn't know how to respond, so I simply stood at attention.

"You wanted to meet with me. I admit I was surprised to hear that was your wish."

He wasn't standing very close, certainly not as close as Zepherin and the gardener.

"I want to know you more," I replied. "If I'm going to be your bride, I wanted to know what you're like."

When he spoke next, there was a cautious smile in his words. "I don't know that you'll like it. I hope you do."

I hated to admit it, but I loved the sound of his voice. It was made to whisper in ears. Every time he spoke, I forgot he was Eros my enemy and I wanted to lean in. "I'm intrigued so far," I said.

"This unusual situation doesn't help. Please, sit."

Zepherin directed me into a seat. It was hard not to picture a long room with Eros and me on opposite sides, shouting at one another, even though our voices were even.

"What do you want to know?" he asked.

Why you let the Eros-suna pollute Aphriso, why you hide instead of admitting that Cytherea should be sole ruler, why you demanded women as your bride...

I pasted a smile on my face. "It must be lonely living up here by yourself. How do you spend your time?"

"I find ways to occupy myself."

"So does every living being." The remark came out of my mouth before I could stop it. A chill crawled down my back. Was a quip like that enough to get me dismissed?

To my surprise, he laughed. "That's true."

"You never go down into the city?"

"No. I doubt I'd be accepted there. Should I go? See the sights?"

This teasing side of Eros surprised me, but it worked to my advantage. "There isn't much to see," I answered.

"No?"

"Unless you like the docks." I hesitated. Boldness won out. "Or the Eros-suna."

Silence.

My insides hardened into a tight ball. I'd said too much. He would know I suspected his real identity, just like Gia had.

"Do you like the Eros-suna?" came his measured response after what seemed like an eternity.

I dragged in a breath, composing myself. How did he want me to answer? "They're all over…"

"But do you enjoy them?" The question bore an edge now.

"I've only gone once," I lied. I knew them only by reputation.

"What are they like?"

"They're…" I racked my mind. "They're places of pleasure."

"Of course they are." He said it almost to himself. "Passion and enjoyment. That sort of thing?"

"Mm. They're wild." *And cheap*. "Sailors like them."

"You don't sound convinced about them. Why have you only gone once?"

"It felt like…" I gripped the seat of the wooden chair, feeling the grain beneath my fingers. This was too far. I was making a mistake. My future was surging away from me.

"Why do you hesitate? Are they so awful?"

I swallowed. "When I think of pleasure, I think of something other than what the Eros-suna can give me."

"Well, that's… Isn't Eros the god of passion? What could be better?" He sounded annoyed.

Did he really not know how the Eros-suna worked?

"Eros is the god of passion," I agreed, "but the Eros-suna don't always align with his ideal of passion and sex." I hurried on to prevent him from responding. "When I want pleasure, I don't want something quick and one-sided with a stranger. I want… I want an ache that builds until I'm trembling before we even touch. I want bodies moving together, drawing out desire and release from all parties. Heated skin, kisses, caresses…"

Eros' voice sounded thick when he responded. "And that's not what you found at the Eros-suna?"

Like a thunderbolt, the thought came too late that Eros, the monster of the mountain, might want to wed a virgin. It was a common enough requirement in the old stories of demigods demanding a bride. Well, there was no use pretending about that one. He'd find out soon enough if he chose me.

"People who choose to... worship that way tend to take what they want quickly." I shrugged. *That's just how it was in the temple too.* I disentangled the idea from my mind. "You could see for yourself if you want to."

A dark chuckle. "Even if we are married?"

"I'm not under any illusions." Surely, he wouldn't keep me after this. I had to salvage this disastrous conversation somehow. "Or do you plan to wed for love, forever?"

The sudden surge of bitterness I felt with the words struck me deep in the chest. Why was I bitter? Did I not believe in love? I believed in pleasure, in Cytherea. Why not love too? Acidic images of Belaria and my uncle and the men behind the temple assaulted me. Lasting love might be a fantasy, but short-term love could be true, at least, couldn't it?

"I hope to love my wife," he answered, a little quieter, his words crisp and honest. "I intend to."

"How? How will you show her?" I injected my voice with all the honey I could muster. "Show me." I held out one hand, inviting him forward. The thick scent in the room cushioned me. I breathed it in.

"I can't show you now," he said with a hint of the same bitterness I felt. "I'm sorry about the Eros-suna. They should be places of more enjoyment than what you describe. Especially for someone like you, who seems to know something about pleasure." His voice took on a seductive quality, though it didn't seem like he intended it. I knew when someone set out to lure a mate with their words. His response was easy, welling up from a true place. Based on the blindfolds and washes and searches, Eros was afraid—a coward—but his sexual allure was innate. In that, he was effortlessly confident.

I didn't know how to respond. "Sometimes I wish they were different," I admitted.

"So do I. I wish things were different."

He wasn't doing a good job of concealing his identity under the guise of a monster.

"Why are you choosing a mate now?" I asked gently. "You've been here for a long time, since before I was born. Did you get lonely here?" I remembered Zepherin and the gardener, still presumably stationed behind me.

A longer pause than the rest.

"Yes. That pleasure you spoke of, that closeness..." His voice trailed off, but the yearning in it twisted my stomach. I knew that feeling too well. Yes, I'd offered pleasure to the goddess at the temple, but that rarely meant a feeling of closeness. Never of belonging. At the temple, I was too violent. In the streets, I was too vulnerable or stubborn or brash. I was always too much and not enough, wedging myself into a corner of community and hoping I could stay.

Cytherea would change that. I would belong with the goddess herself.

"I want that too," I confessed. "My parents sent me here, but if you will show me kindness..."

"And generosity, and good sex?" His hoarse, joking tone sent shivers up my back.

"Yes," I laughed. "Then maybe we can both find it."

He hummed, a guttural sound.

"So, where are we?" I asked. We'd walked from the women's quarters down the vinegar hallway, taken a right-hand turn, and ended up here. I could find my way again if I had to.

"Will it alarm you if I say my personal quarters?"

My heart jumped. I'd hardly dared to hope for this much luck. "Are you afraid someone would see us if we walked together?" I teased.

"You... can't see." Thick regret laced his sultry voice.

"You could lead me, hold my hand. Or we could stay here, if you prefer." I stopped myself from biting my lip to keep from saying more. This wasn't the temple. Would all my bold comments tip him off about my true intentions? What kind of person desperately wanted to wed a monster? No one. Unless they knew he wasn't a creature at all, but the demi-god of lust, Eros.

He seemed to have the same thought, because he didn't answer. I heard Zepherin breathing quietly behind me. The musky smell in the room made my head spin with visions of how I could bend him to choose me over the others.

Inwardly cursing myself, I held the chaotic part inside me at bay. At my core, I was desperate. Always desperate—for safety, for pleasure, for belonging. And Eros was my gateway to those things, as long as he didn't detect the desperate woman underneath.

His silence suggested that he did.

I forced myself to wait.

"I wish I could," he said, quiet and raspy.

This was as private as any conversation could be with the demi-god. With other amazing women like Cressida in the mix, I had to seize my chance now, even if it did make me seem like a temple courtesan or an Eros-suna devotee.

"You can't touch me? Are you shy around women, monster of the mountain?"

A series of taps told me he was drumming his fingers on something, maybe armrests. "No."

"To both questions...?" I tilted my head. "What should I call you? I can't call you the creature. You don't seem like a beastly creature to me."

"Call me... Him."

"Like you're the only male?" I purred.

A shuffle. "Psyche." My name sounded very good in that voice of his. "Why do you want me to choose you this much?"

"*Don't* you want to choose me?"

No answer. This was a test. I had to answer his question first.

"I want a new life," I admitted, "to get away. My parents gave me up." I thought of Belaria and my uncle. "Who would want to stay where they aren't wanted? And you've been generous since we've arrived here. You're a demi-god. Our children would be demi-gods. And I like the sound of your voice, like I said." I finished my explanation with a smile.

"Psyche..."

With that one word, I felt my hopes slipping away. Panic circled my chest. "I choose you," I said. "I know you're afraid and alone up here. You don't want to be touched. But I choose you, and I hope you'll choose me." All I needed was one more encounter with Eros. If Cytherea gave me the knife, I could end him. Too bad that tantalizing presence had to go. I still hated him for many reasons, but this room exuded sensuality that I craved. Nothing like those lecherous sailors at the temple.

I held out my hand again. When it hovered in empty air, I licked my palm in one suggestive sweep. "See? Nothing to harm you."

After a few seconds, "My lord." Zepherin muttered it quickly, a warning.

What was Eros doing? Were my words working? Normally, I could use my physical assets to seduce, not just verbal persuasion. Pride surged up inside me, small and warm. I could do this.

"That's all right. You don't have to touch me if you don't want to," I said. "But would you... would you like me to do it?"

"Don't come over here." Eros again, commanding this time, though I heard a tinge of fear too. There was something forced in the way he said it, as though he were commanding himself too.

A smirk played on my lips. "I won't. I could stay here. Or..." I swiveled my head, though I couldn't see anything. "This is your personal room? There's a bed, isn't there? Would you let me get on it?"

In the following silence, I imagined the three males in the room conversing with their eyes. Zepherin would no doubt be visibly nervous.

"Zepherin and Olitor are here," Eros reminded me.

"I know. They can watch too."

"Watch." Eros repeated the word in a whisper, almost to

himself. If he were really the lord of sex and passion, he understood me perfectly. His next order was breathless. "Lead her to the bed."

The place where Eros slept every night. The exact location where I could end his life.

Hope welled inside me.

Zepherin obeyed, setting his hand on my shoulder as I rose. The room wasn't as large as I had supposed at first. The bed was only a few steps away.

I crawled atop the large mattress before turning to face the area where Eros had been. The blankets were deep and soft, better than any I'd ever slept in. And the smell... If the rest of the room smelled like damp plant life and sweet juices, the bed smelled mouthwateringly masculine. A heightened version of what I'd sensed before. I could snuggle into these covers and stay for days.

I let out a pleased moan as I sat back. "This bed," I exclaimed. "It's heavenly!"

"Even more so now," Eros said.

I didn't have to force my smile. "Imagine what we could do here." I parted my legs suggestively, drawing out the motion. I drew my skirt above my knees so it rode up around my hips when I spread wider. My legs were bare. The sensation of naked skin against the blankets was divine.

Wouldn't the worshippers of Eros be jealous?

I shoved away the thought and focused on the alluring odors and the audible breathing of the demi-gods watching me. Eros's innate sexuality that infused this room. Bit by bit, I guided my hand over my knee and across my bare thigh, tracing a slow path to my core. I'd make them wait, make them want this.

Images of the best sexual encounters I'd had paraded through my mind—some real, some imaginary—until I started to pulse, anticipatory. The panties I wore provided a thin barrier. Maybe they could see me getting wetter as I prodded the first finger against the fabric, just a light touch.

I imagined the fingers were a kind, eager lover's, teasing. Somebody who saw me and wanted me, who knew what turned me on, who reveled in their ability to enflame every nerve before finally giving me what I craved.

I imagined the hand belonged to Eros, demi-god of seduction.

Nerves alighting with a familiar keen ache, I traced my lines a little more firmly as I swelled and grew slick. Those soft touches were enough to make my breathing shallow.

Leaning back on an elbow, I moved the panties aside and threaded my finger through the stiff hair. I knew the spots I liked, but finding them was still a matter for exploration. I groaned, still more theatrical than authentic, and rubbed along the ridge.

It didn't take me long to find a rhythm. The invisible watchers faded. All my focus narrowed to the places my fingers touched, pressing hard on my clit, teasing my entrance, rubbing the mound... My fingers got wetter as the friction coaxed pleasure from me. The only sounds I heard some would call obscene. My grunts weren't staged now, but urgent.

Finally, I lay back so my other hand could finish, working multiple places at once. The ache between my legs spiked out to other parts of my body. I spasmed, close to the edge. With a final surge, not a full little death, but close, my stomach contracted and released.

My panting became a sigh. I replaced my underwear, though it was soaked through, and pulled my dress down again as I sat up.

No one said anything.

At least I'd found some relief and given Eros a show. Hopefully, I tempted him to select me as his bride.

I scooted to the edge of the bed. "I might have gotten something wet," I said softly, not quite an apology.

At last, a long intake of breath. "Take her out."

Shit. I'd let the wrong part of me decide on tactics. "If I've done..."

"Just take her out."

A hand once again clamped on my shoulder, hotter this time, or maybe that was my own flushed skin. Zepherin and the gardener's slightly uneven breathing followed me out of the seductive room into the cool, antiseptic hallway as we headed back.

12

EROS

O*h.*

My.

Gods.

I'd had sex a hundred ways, but Psyche made me imagine a hundred more. I worked furiously at my rock-hard cock, aching for that sweet, slippery entrance but having to settle for my own hand. I was the only partner I'd had for decades. I missed the push and pull, the slide inside, the abandon of release when my lover contracted around me, mouth ratcheting open. But this was all I could do for now, and I had to do something. I feared I might burst just watching her.

Psyche's mischievous smirk flashed behind my closed lids. The image of her perfect body sprawled on my covers brought me to the brink, the tension so thick it hurt. I only lasted seconds. With a sharp exhale, I crested, vision turning white, and spilled out.

When I came to, I realized I made a mess on the floor. Still heaving in breaths, I shoved myself back in my pants and stood shakily to my feet. My mind stirred hazily as I moved automatically to wipe it up.

There's more to a divine marriage than sex. But the logical thought bounced off my consciousness. Even before Psyche crawled onto my bed, I'd felt drawn to her. She was the only one who explicitly asked to meet with me. It had been so long since anyone requested to talk to me. And then for her to awaken my lust so brazenly... It reminded me of days before all this danger and fear.

When I was young, my mother largely ignored me except to show me off. I admired her, but she didn't know the first thing about me, except that I was beautiful. She made me feel like a doll or a trophy. Once, I caught a hare and placed it under a serving dish to startle her. I thought she might laugh. When the creature jumped out, she raged at me and demanded that I not leave her side for a week so I couldn't "wander off." During that whole week, she didn't say a single word to me.

It was just the two of us most of the time, so loneliness settled like rust in my bones. It didn't matter how many people I met. It didn't matter who admired my body. It didn't even matter how many people I bedded. In fact, the more people I encountered, the colder my mother became. It was as though she wanted to punish me by keeping me tethered to her side forever.

At first, I tried to appease her. I stopped playing harmless tricks. For a while, I even denied myself sexual companions, releasing all my frustrated energy into relentless hours of archery practice. I became a very good shot, both on the ground and in the air, but I couldn't deny what I was—the demi-god lust. No amount of physical training could quell the growing ache within me to experience more of the world.

I didn't want to be sheltered. I wanted to live.

Primal urges led me to grab at pleasure wherever I could get it. I felt unleashed, like every day was a celebration. And it was. A celebration of life. Nothing excited me more than wringing every drop of desire out of my partners. And I was damn good at it. Every wild exchange drowned my latent loneliness in a wave of blissful unconsciousness. In their arms, I felt wanted.

And then they would leave or I would leave, and I'd start again.

Only in the past few years had I finally understood that sex would never lead to the belonging I craved. I wanted both. *Gods*, I wanted both. My lust ran as deep as my loneliness.

In Silkuoma, at least I could satisfy one.

Psyche tempted me to believe in the impossible again, but I knew I couldn't follow that song or else I'd smash against the rocks of reality. Maybe this time I wouldn't survive.

Should I risk that level of pain? I knew I was gullible. I knew I was prone to dreaming, even if it was only on behalf of somebody else. But I longed so desperately for intimacy—*true* intimacy—that a rock formed in my throat.

If only I had more time to decide...

The eclipse was coming, whether I wanted it to or not, hedging me in, drawing yet another rope around me when I already felt stuffed into a suffocating box. If I missed this deadline, I'd have to endure another ten years of uncertainty and threat. With dozens of near misses, I doubted I could last that long. At some point, Cytherea would find my hiding place.

Maybe it would be safer to choose someone else. My first impressions of all the women were positive. They were unique and beautiful. No one else had made me frantically reach inside my pants, though.

Psyche's confidence intoxicated me. Even from across the room, I could sense her heated skin, the speed of her breathing, and I wanted to swallow it all, to order the others from the room so we could mold together like we both wanted to. And then when she got on the bed, I couldn't breathe. I had flushed hot, growing painfully hard. And that was before she leaned into her own pleasure.

In a small corner of my mind, I remembered that Zepherin and Olitor were there. Well, if there was one way to push them into each other's arms, this would do it.

I was dumbstruck. Psyche spreading her legs on my blankets was a sight I wouldn't soon forget. If ever. And when she pulled aside her underwear, kneading that pink pussy with her fingers... My *gods*!

The memory brought blood rushing to my cock again. I couldn't think coherently this way. I needed to choose a partner for life and all I could picture was doing to Psyche what she had done to herself. The way she would arch against me, the way she would—

I growled. Time was running out. Time was running out. I repeated it to myself over and over until I started to understand the truth of it. These women weren't here for some kind of orgy. They were here so I could choose one who wasn't in league with the goddess so I could finally come out from beneath her clutches, so I could fly again without fear.

So I could live.

Psyche's presence engulfed me like a wildfire. I couldn't think straight under those conditions. And I couldn't survive the heartbreak if I let it burn.

Exhaling a deep sigh, I wrenched my thoughts toward the upcoming meetings with the others.

I would choose one of them.

Who was next?

❦ 13 ❦

PSYCHE

Xanthi went next. She didn't appear afraid when Zepherin tied the blindfold over her eyes. Her freckled skin even looked flushed with excitement. Seeing her leave with Zepherin and the handsome gardener (I'd been right) left my stomach in knots.

Despite what I'd done in front of Eros earlier, I couldn't fall asleep after Xanthi left. I wanted to hear how her meeting went. If I still had a chance or if Eros had written me off as a potential bride.

He kicked me out. Did that mean I'd angered him? That he'd seen beneath my desperation to the truth? Surely the demi-god of lust didn't have delicate sensibilities that would be bothered by what I'd done. Zepherin and the gardener, on the other hand...

Imagining their reactions made me smirk into the darkness. Surely, they couldn't be scandalized by me if they served Eros himself. However, Zepherin's hoarse voice when he'd dropped me off at my room said otherwise.

Along the seaport and in the temple, almost everyone was open about sexuality, both their own and others'. Sometimes too much. The openness gave predators permission—in their minds—to overpower whoever they wanted.

My smile faded.

Faint light from beneath the door revealed the lumpy shadows of the bed next to mine.

"Cressida, are you awake?"

She stirred, raising one long arm into the slice of light. With a groan, she rolled to face me. "Finally ready to tell your story?" she slurred, grumpy.

That wasn't my intention for waking her. I'd merely wanted company.

"I... um... Sure." I would leave out the more salacious parts of the story, but they all deserved to know. My face heated with shame that I hadn't told Xanthi more before she left. Just because I needed to ultimately win this bridal contest didn't mean I wished any of them ill will. They were all nervous too, although for different reasons. The least I could do was tell them some of what I knew to calm their nerves. "Let's call Stantina and Cybel in here too."

She sighed. "Or we could just meet in the common area and wait for Xanthi at this point. Unless he keeps her for the night."

I didn't contradict her, but I would have bet my right arm that Eros wouldn't spend the night with Xanthi, no matter how much he might like her.

"All right." I rolled quickly out of bed, agitation living in my limbs.

"Psyche," Cressida moaned, lifting her arm again.

I took it and hauled her to her feet. She was warm with sleep. Before we exited, she shook herself and inhabited the version of her that we saw most often—cynical, strong, and ready to shut down any bullshit. I watched her stalk over to the bedroom door on the other side of the cool room with something like wonder. She'd endured so much, but beneath the surface dwelled a warrior, a defender.

I was glad she welcomed the others. On the first night, she'd complained about some of the others crying. Maybe that was because she had been trying not to herself.

Cybel looked like a bronze statue even mussed with the early stages of sleep. Lanterns backlit her blonde hair, burning wayward lines of it white.

Stantina, with her round face and petite figure, padded along behind them, nibbling on the rare berries she'd requested. She wore a fluffy, gold-threaded robe, also part of her present from Eros, I guessed.

"Psyche," Cressida announced, "is going to tell us everything."

Stantina shivered once with surprise, pausing her chewing.

"About your meeting with...?" Cybel asked.

"Yes."

We all sat. Their postures reminded me forcefully of listening to my guardian tell ghost stories to a group of us children. I couldn't remember the specific occasion. It was more of a feeling. The smell of tall grass, pebbles digging into my bare calves as I sat cross-legged with the others. Chills running down our spine as shadows lengthened.

"He didn't allow me to see him," I began.

Cybel nodded her graceful neck while Cressida muttered, "Obviously. Prick."

I glanced sideways at her. "So I don't know what he looks like, but Zepherin took me to what I think was his room."

"Zepherin's?" Cressida asked, incredulous.

"The... *Him*. The one considering us." I wanted desperately to say his name, to stop all this stupid vagueness.

"You went to his room?" Stantina's eyes rounded. "What did he do?" Fear laced her words like liquor in juice.

"He just talked." I did a little more than just talk, but I wouldn't tell them that. "We had a conversation. A little longer than our first meeting."

"You came back pretty quickly, though," Cressida put in, now clearly more interested in what I was saying.

"He's... a man of few words."

"Man?" Cressida repeated.

"Or demi-god, I guess. A male of few words. But our conversation was good, actually. I think he was honest with me, and I think he's really looking for a loving relationship." My mouth almost tripped on the final words. That was absurd, wasn't it? Or maybe pathetic, but it was hard to think so when I yearned for that too. I suppose I'd simply given up on that idea a long time ago. I could find pleasure and offer it to the goddess. That was enough for me. Until it wasn't.

"Love?" Cressida scoffed. "I kidnap all my potential lovers too. Don't you, Psyche?"

The corner of Cybel's mouth creased, but Stantina merely looked worried.

I focused on Stantina, who fought deeper fear than any of us. "He doesn't seem vicious. I think he wants whoever he chooses to *want him* as well." A surprisingly thoughtful idea, for a demi-god.

I laughed at my own thought. If that was thoughtful, then the criteria for kindness had reached a low point. Maybe I was farther gone than I thought.

And lonelier than I thought.

"He's just lonely?" Cybel guessed.

My belly somersaulted at the echo. "Yes."

"So, when we leave, he doesn't...?"

"I don't think so." Demi-gods were famously fickle, though, so I didn't want to make promises on his behalf.

Stantina released a breath and went on eating her berries. "What did you talk about?"

Although her shoulders still held tension, she looked relieved.

"Oh..." I pretended to recall. "It was just about what we're each looking for in a mate, what we like to do, that kind of thing. All boring, really."

"What *are* you looking for?" Cressida eyed me suspiciously.

I applauded myself for not squirming under her scrutiny. I didn't want to lie to her, to any of them. "In a mate?"

"No, in the perfect breakfast," she rejoined, deadpan.

Stantina and Cybel stared with open curiosity too.

"It's not like I can choose..." I hedged again.

"We talked about this," Cressida said, cocking her eyebrows meaningfully. Just because we were comfortable in this moment didn't mean she could start talking about rejecting Eros in the open. I was glad she understood there were some boundaries she shouldn't cross, just in case Eros did have the typical deathless volatility lying beneath his skin.

"What did you tell him?" Cybel coaxed.

"That I want someone kind. Generous." I nodded at Stantina's berries. Hers were the only gifts I'd seen so far, and I'd witnessed several being dropped off at her door: rare jewels, delicacies, and golden outfits. Good for her for having the guts to ask. I ought to do the same. Cressida had requested nothing, maybe out of protest.

"What about you, Stantina?" I asked.

"Me?" She laid a delicate hand on her chest. She dropped her eyes. "I don't know..."

"You have to have thought about it," Cressida pressed.

"Not really." Her voice went so quiet that I was about to apologize when she said, "Kind sounds nice. Someone who wants me."

I could tell she was thinking of someone in particular. My stomach knotted.

"Someone who listens," she went on, still looking at the floor. "Someone who thinks I'm beautiful and doesn't hurt me." She chewed her full bottom lip. Blinking a couple times, she finally looked back up at me. "If I could have anything, I'd want that."

I held her gaze. "You deserve *at least* that, Stantina." I hadn't spent much time with her, but whenever I did, she was conscientious and thoughtful, with a deep core of bravery she accessed whenever she felt fear. Despite seeming timid, she would be a difficult woman to break. I found myself liking her more and more.

"Did someone hurt you?" Cressida's question came out gentle. I had a vision of Cressida fighting on behalf of women who, like her, had been treated like nothing. My heart swelled.

After a moment, Stantina gave a small nod. "I was married."

"Married?" I whispered, shocked. I had assumed that all these women had never been married, that most might even be virgins.

"For two years." She didn't look older than me. "And then he gave me back to my parents. Said I... I wasn't worth the trouble." She glanced at the final berry in her hand, her forehead creasing with obvious guilt.

"No," I said, kneeling in front of her and taking her hands between mine. I stared into her face and wished her husband were here so I could exact vengeance on him too. "You deserve love. You deserve to ask for berries and cakes and silk and gold. The monster can afford it. Ask for the whole gods-damned castle! And fuck your husband!"

Cybel inhaled sharply at my outburst, but I wasn't finished. I'd entered a gray area between my assumed identity of a helpless bridal sacrifice and my real one. The woman with chaos in her soul and unknowns in her future, but a woman who knew what love *wasn't*.

"May he rot in Abaddon for what he did to you. You know what kind of mate I'd choose for you? I'd choose someone who loves to listen to your voice, who smooths your hair down every night, who cooks you delicacies and lets you curl up in his lap, who laughs at your jokes. Someone gorgeous who loves to pleasure you. He'd be rich and never ignore someone truly in need. I'd choose a man who knows every part of your past and admires you anyway."

I stopped myself. My eyes were wet.

Stantina blinked away tears as well.

I'd said too much. My rant turned into a piece of my soul, as if I'd been forced inside out. These were some of my deepest longings. Maybe I hadn't even been talking about Stantina by the end. Only myself.

I cleared my throat and sat back on my heels. "So," I said hoarsely, "either you'll be chosen and doted on as a demi-god's wife, or you'll go back home where *you* get to make the choice. Don't settle for piece of shit like your husband. Better to run to Nalia or something if you can. At least there you'll be free."

Tears still clung to my lashes.

She nodded stoutly at me.

"We all deserve a choice," Cressida agreed from behind me.

Footsteps hushed us. Three pairs.

In moments, Xanthi returned, blindfolded, ushered in by Zepherin and the gardener. Her flushed cheeks showed off her freckles when Zepherin undid the knot and released the blindfold.

I didn't have time to react before Cressida marched up to Zepherin as she had done the other day.

Don't say something that will get you in trouble! I clenched my fists in my lap, still crouching in front of Stantina and Cybel.

"We have a few more requests," she said.

Zepherin wrapped the blindfold around his hand before stuffing it in a pocket. "What do you need?"

Xanthi didn't move to join us, listening instead to Cressida.

"We *need* a little dignity." She glanced down at the pocket where Zepherin had stowed the piece of cloth. She didn't need to look far. Zepherin was so much taller than the rest of us. "But what we want is meat and cheese and berries and cream. Enough for all of us."

From the corner of my eye, I saw Stantina's mouth twitch with apprehensive amusement.

Zepherin scanned us as if counting, his expression uncharacteristically unreadable. "That will be no trouble at all. He has said you ladies can ask for whatever you wish."

"That's what we wish for at this moment."

"And wine, please!" Cybel cried.

I grinned.

A ghost of irritation passed over Zepherin's features. "I'll bring it up. And, Cressida, he wants to meet with you tomorrow. I'll come and get you when it's time." With that, he turned and stalked away, the line of his strong back taut with tension.

Cressida led Xanthi back to the group. Her beautiful face was full of questions and Cressida didn't answer right away.

Stantina exhaled. "I thought they would dismiss me."

"Why?" I asked.

She blushed. "Because I asked for all this."

No, she could ask for much more and Eros would still provide it for her. I had no idea why I felt so sure. We'd had two brief conversations. And he was, at heart, a selfish and depraved being, right?

Another low bar for goodness. Or was it? I hadn't lied when I said I appreciated generosity in a partner.

Looking around at the other women, an uncomfortable feeling churned in my gut. I was selfish too, because I wanted more than a quiet, peaceful existence in the mighty Cytherea's shadow. I yearned for that peace, yes, but I wanted love. I wanted *this*.

Maybe when I completed my mission and earned the

goddess's reward, I'd meet a former courtesan like Castor. (I usually preferred males as sexual companions, when they weren't pricks.) We'd live a happy, simple life together far from strife. He would listen and think I was beautiful, and he wouldn't hurt me.

I swallowed around the lump in my throat. In the recesses of my soul, I thought that was the most I could possibly deserve.

But as the five of us sat together eating spoonfuls of berries and cream, my mind kept drifting to statues of Eros and the longing in his voice and the smell of his room.

14

EROS

Cressida frowned at me. Perhaps it wasn't a full frown. It was like the look Zepherin got when I displeased him with a command. Lines around the mouth, a certain stiffness.

I couldn't see her eyes, of course, but it wasn't difficult to imagine that they frowned too.

She sat in the same chair as the other girls, a body length away from me. Her heart beat a steady rhythm. Just a little fast.

Cressida was my last visit.

I flexed my wings as quietly as I could, trying not to ruffle the plants behind me. "How have you found your accommodations?"

Inwardly, I groaned. I wasn't a diplomat, but I sounded like the gods who used to visit my mother when I was a child. They'd smile and start out saying bland, proper things that made me itch to leave. My mother could stand those pleasantries longer than I could, but she rarely partook in them, which I admired her for. Through example, she taught me to ask for what I wanted, to make people feel good, to seduce.

I hadn't used those talents in a long time. I feared I was woefully out of practice.

"They're fine," came Cressida's curt reply. "We enjoyed the berries and cream the other night."

I smiled. Even Zepherin's face softened from its typical expression of looking put out.

Imagining the ladies all together finding joy in each other's company squeezed my heart pleasantly. I ran over them all in my head. Snagged on Psyche. Her words and actions echoed in my mind during the day and especially at night when I was trying to sleep. I didn't want to compare all the others to her. Each girl was brilliant in her own way. I enjoyed all of them. By habit, I considered which would make good matches, for me or each other.

"I could bring more to you," I said.

"Okay." After a pause, she asked, "How do you do all that?"

"All what?"

"Get us berries and cream or whatever we want? Do you have everything here waiting?" A slight hitch in her voice betrayed sudden nerves, as if I would think her a thief. But her hesitation lasted only a moment before she tucked it away.

"Demi-gods all have ways to get such things. Zepherin is happy to serve." I cast him a cheeky look where he stood beside Olitor. He glowered back.

"Has he always served you?"

Zepherin's pulse kicked a little higher. He didn't like to talk about the circumstances of our arrangement, and neither did I.

"Always? No."

Awkward silence fell between us. I studied her. Her curiosity intrigued me, and she had a tantalizing indentation in her bottom lip. It was a soft spot in an otherwise rigid exterior. She was thin and strong, echoing the strength within. Even though she had been upset ever since she sat down, I felt it would only take the right touch to open her up.

But I couldn't touch her. And my verbal sex appeal had dried up to almost nothing from lack of practice.

With Zepherin and Olitor standing guard behind her, three faces set in mild accusation, I couldn't help but grow surly too. It was like they were ganging up on me. Olitor kept his smooth face carefully neutral, but Zepherin and Cressida clearly harbored annoyance.

My skin heated. I kept this room too hot. For a moment, I had felt the confines of my rules relax, but now they seemed to snap back into place.

Fold the gloves. Cover them with the hare-spotted cloth.

Strap in the wings.

Cover yourself with the cloak until you can't see.

Don't go outside unless it's somewhere no one can see you. Definitely don't go to Card, where the Eros-suna have become harmful.

I hadn't known about that last part, and now it was yet another thing this threat prohibited me from fixing. I couldn't fix anything. If the people's worship drove Cytherea's attempts on my life, at least that worship should enrich humans' lives, not steal from them. Was I living this way for nothing?

I had only visited Card once, long before Eros-suna had cropped up there. I remembered it as somewhere pleasant, but not interesting enough to visit again. Evidently, things had changed. Psyche's expression and temperature as she skirted around the topic of my cult told me more than her words. The Eros-suna had to be stopped, changed. I'd been so busy trying to save my own skin that I hadn't even considered them. If Psyche hadn't brought this to my attention...

I drummed my fingers against the armrest of my chair. *Breathe in. Breathe out.*

"My lord," Cressida said, slowly, "you didn't answer either of my questions."

My brow furrowed as my attention snapped back to her. "Didn't I?" The words came out too sharp.

Zepherin narrowed his eyes, whether to admonish me for my tone or warn me not to answer questions about him, I didn't know.

"No, you didn't," she pressed.

The ghost of a smile passed Zepherin's lips as he glanced down at her. Of course he would like to see someone else push back against me.

I ran rough fingers through my hair. How could I blame her—either of them? The least I could do was calm her fears and try to see beneath the hard surface. "I'm sorry. Except for these past few days with you five, I've been out of practice speaking to anyone. Zepherin, why don't you answer her question?"

His quick gaze darkened.

Cressida twisted in her seat as if she could see him. "Were you... invited, too?"

I winced at the implication. I demanded potential brides to join me. Did I demand his service too?

There were many ways to be trapped.

I almost regretted sending him the question. Now, he had no choice but to answer in a way that didn't reveal my identity.

I clenched my teeth in my mouth. I couldn't afford to alienate Zepherin any further. He was one of my only remaining friends. If I could call him a friend at all, the way I treated him.

I thought again of the women and their dessert. *That* was what friendship looked like, at least the way I pictured it. My past told me that kind of easiness wasn't a fantasy. *That* was the ingredient I wanted in a partner beyond sexual chemistry. I was Eros. Even if my words sounded rusty, once I touched my wife, I knew I'd find sexual chemistry. The other was harder to find.

I wrenched my thoughts back to Cressida and the others before a whirlpool of Psyche-related thoughts consumed me.

"Many demi-gods have provinces," he began. "I'm a soldier in his." He caught my eye. *Was* a soldier, but he didn't correct himself. "I joined about fifty years ago."

Cressida's lovely mouth opened in surprise. Humans lived for so short a time.

Zepherin served my small army from right before the first attempt on my life: the honey tea. I counted time in attacks.

"Now you're his personal guard?" Cressida asked. The blindfold rose as though she were raising her eyebrows with open skepticism.

Now it was my turn to give a little smirk. Even Olitor, normally so stoic, glanced sideways at him.

Zepherin blushed.

I'd seen him gruff, earnest, naïve, resigned, but never blushing. My plan was working. Despite all the struggle of the past decades, I loved nothing more than witnessing people fall for each other.

"Sort of," Zepherin answered.

Already, I was plotting more ways to stick them in situations together. Damn, I was good at this. Now, if I could be good at it for myself too...

"He serves me well," I cut in. No need to force him to tell more of the story.

Attack #4: the frontal assault. Cytherea sent some of her army to Silkuoma to eliminate me. Demi-gods and humans fought and died on the steps of my palace. All of Zepherin's regiment fell. Except him. Because he ran.

I forced him to make up for it ever since. Because I showed him mercy, he owed me allegiance. Maybe, after a few more decades, he could atone for leaving his brothers and sisters behind. Fuck, he already had atoned for it, but I couldn't beat the thought of him leaving. When the attack happened, he was the youngest member of the regiment, barely old enough to serve. No wonder he was frightened. We'd never breached the subject again after I found him hiding in a sea cave.

Even now, regret clouded his eyes when he thought I wasn't looking at him. But I was always looking. Anyone could be a threat to me. Even my fierce, innocent Zepherin.

Cressida made a noise that suggested she was unconvinced.

I liked her. She made it easy to talk. Or at least, not hard. Stantina was so hesitant that any conversation bordered on those empty chats my mother and her deathless guests used to have. I wanted to talk about what these women were passionate about, what made their blood heat, but I no longer knew how.

I needed time to learn how to charm people again. My words had broken from swirling again and again and again in my own head with no outlet.

No wonder I didn't consider the Eros-suna.

No wonder I didn't let Zepherin leave.

No wonder I was so godsdamned selfish sometimes. And no wonder I couldn't say what I wanted to.

My words struggled against the bars of my fear and lust. The eclipse was coming. I had to find some way to choose a bride.

After almost an hour with Cressida, I dismissed her, invigorated by an idea. I dug around for pen and parchment. I'd write each woman a letter. That wasn't usually my style, but my style couldn't happen with so much room between us. This way, time and focus were on my side. I could consider flirtations to allure them and questions to help me make my ultimate decision.

I bent over a stack of paper, pen poised. When was the last time I'd written a letter? Oh yes. It was an answer to a noble couple in Silkuoma inviting me to join them for a... celebration. All the ships in their fishing business had survived a massive storm. They wanted a taste of what I could offer. It was a fun night. They were so happy and relieved they hadn't lost everything, and I taught them the ways of the palace.

I shook off the memory. That wasn't my life anymore. I would choose one woman. If she wanted us to be exclusively faithful to each another, I'd honor that. That was a new kind of intimacy for me.

Intimacy—there was that bubble of hope again. That stupid voice that said, *What if she loves you?* I locked away those thoughts for another time. Whether or not my wife loved me in the way I craved, there were five impressive women here, and they all deserved attention.

Cressida was smart but a little acidic. With time, we could be a good match. Her answers were short, but who in her position wouldn't be resentful of the circumstances that had brought them here? I wished I could tell her it would be all right, to show her my true face and quiet her fears.

Stantina was quiet, submissive. After all this time alone, I wanted my mate to talk to me. I wanted companionship in every sense of the word, and Stantina needed time to open up.

Cybel put on a brave face, but she was clearly edgy in my presence. If I'd been able to interact with her in my true form, I could have put her at ease. As the creature of the mountain, however, I didn't have all my powers at my disposal.

Xanthi engaged in conversation, reaching for some crumb of goodness in me. With all the questions she asked, it felt almost like a game.

None of them fascinated me like Psyche did. Whenever we talked, I wanted to lean in. There was something mysterious about her, even though she was more open about her life—and her body—than the others. She was the only one who asked if I was lonely.

I had to be sure, and I couldn't be sure about my choice while Psyche was making those unholy noises, spread wide like a dish to feast on. I had only a few days left, and I had to use them to determine if Psyche was a threat—a deliciously tantalizing threat, but a threat nonetheless. Her interest in me was too intense. I began with her.

Psyche, I wrote, *I'm sorry for making you leave my chambers so soon. Your actions made me lose my head and need certain relief that I didn't want everyone to witness. Given what you did, I doubt you would have minded overhearing what I did next. Maybe isolation has made me squeamish.*

I chuckled to myself. If anything, my desires raged just as hotly as before. But, with no outlet apart from myself, racy dreams filled my mind more insistently. Back home, I'd bedded multiple gods and humans at once, sometimes. Now, to be naked in anyone else's presence was to be at risk. To be in anyone else's presence *at all* was a risk. *Fucking Cytherea...*

I poised the pen again. *Forgive me, you fascinating creature.* My instinct was to tell Psyche how she kept me spellbound and lure her back with poetic promises of what I'd do with her body. But this wasn't a typical romantic entanglement. This was for life. Eternal life, if I wasn't killed. So I crammed the chaos within into a corner and tried to be strategic.

I have two questions, I wrote. *First, if I asked you to be my bride, would you be content to say yes? And then, what do you think I look like? Please be specific about the image in your head, even if it's dreadful. It torments me that you might flee when you know the truth.*

My torment wasn't that she would flee, but that Cytherea would get to her and Psyche would catch me off guard. Pothos all over again.

But I couldn't say any of that.

Because Cytherea controlled even my words.

I will choose a wife soon, but I will do my best to answer any question you ask if you reply quickly. Rubbing my lips together, I added, *Whether it's with me or another, I hope you find love to quell your loneliness too. If it's with me, and your question relates to what happened in my bedroom, the answer will be yes before you finish asking the question.*

I signed the letter *Affectionately, Him* and sealed it with wax.

I paced for a minute before sitting down to write the next four letters. Each one needed consideration. Each woman could be the key to my godhood and, I increasingly hoped, true intimate companionship. I thought of it more than I thought about the impending ceremony.

Once I finished writing the letters expressing my attraction and comfort and questions, I tied the stack with ribbon. It was late. The women would most likely be sleeping. Would it be so bad if I delivered these myself, saw how well Zepherin took care of them? I wouldn't get close. I'd simply leave the letters where they could find them tomorrow.

With practiced movements, I bound my wings against my aching back, tugged on the gloves, and pulled the huge cloak over my form before sweeping from the room.

15

PSYCHE

Cressida still wasn't back yet.

My lungs constricted. How would she act around him? She would never copy what I'd done, even if I'd told her about it. She didn't want to become the monster's wife. No need to seduce someone she didn't want. But she'd been so brash with Zepherin earlier. Would Eros punish her if she spoke her mind with him too?

No, he wouldn't. I'd been incredibly forward and he hadn't punished me.

Except to kick me out. Angrily.

I gripped my rough sheets in two fists. Nerves twisted in my belly, but I couldn't pinpoint the exact cause. Cressida, Eros, the goddess... even myself. There was a lot to worry about.

I exhaled slowly, as Kalli had taught me to do after a particularly rough night. Our deep breathing exercises never failed to set me on a better course.

Why did he show that slight uncertainty when he'd asked why I was so intent on winning him? Did he suspect the truth?

If he looked like the little statues of him his devotees in Card didn't even try to hide, then he had no reason to feel insecure about procuring partners. His voice and scent conjured images of sculpted muscles, an effortlessly erotic stance, ready lips. He represented experience and innocence at once. I hated what he had done to the city, but I'd be lying if I said I wouldn't look forward to tasting his body if we had to wed. If I got that far.

Cressida had to be finished with her one-on-one time by now. Hours had passed.

I cocked my ear to listen, but the only sounds in the main area were the occasional drones of insects as they buzzed around the wall of plants.

All these growing things, both in our area and in Eros' personal room. Like he wanted something alive to be near him. Eros had been in hiding so long, he must miss all the company he gave up to be on the run. And for what? The worship he demanded that belonged to the true queen? How selfish and cowardly!

If Cressida *wasn't* with Eros anymore, then was he alone? In the room I knew how to find?

My skin buzzed. What if…?

I sat up in bed. Cytherea had said she'd find me and provide me with a knife. Maybe I didn't have to wait to see if Eros chose me among these other women. In fact, that could be much better. Xanthi was energized after her visit with Eros, practically glowing. Stantina's fears abated after her meeting. She spoke of him almost with awe. Cybel was the only one who didn't come back fairly certain she would be chosen as his bride. Either Eros had a way of winning people over or he really was attracted to all of us. I couldn't count on him choosing me. No one else had been dismissed as abruptly. I'd asked. Xanthi looked at me with sympathy now.

Also, we still didn't know what had happened to Gia and the rest. If they were being killed off one by one—when had I stopped believing that was the case?—then it was better to end this now before more innocent people got hurt.

Or, more likely, before Eros married someone else.

"Queen Cytherea," I whispered into the dark. Despite all my time in her temple, I didn't know how to summon her. I didn't even know if she could be summoned. But I was alone now. It was the perfect time to deposit that knife in my hand. "I'm ready."

I waited.

And waited.

And waited.

Nothing happened.

Did I have to be somewhere else, somewhere easier to appear in and out of?

I stood and padded to the door, listening again for any movement. Nothing. Opening the door a crack, I peered out. The common area appeared empty.

I slipped out, shutting the door behind me. Summer heat didn't warm this cavernous area like it did Eros's room. Instead, cool air wrapped around my bare legs.

"Queen Cytherea," I mouthed. No sign of the gardener, of the women, of anyone, but I still had to be cautious. If Eros learned I was calling to his enemy, I'd be dead. No amount of flirting and goodwill negated the fact that he was deathless and I was a human meddling in the affairs of gods.

Feeling foolish, I held out my hands. Unsurprisingly, a knife didn't magically drop into them. Too bad *I* wasn't a demi-god. Then I could walk through the air as Zepherin had done with us on the cliffside and fetch one myself.

A tiny noise, like someone exhaling, set my skin tingling. My spine stiffening with nerves, I listened hard.

I hadn't imagined it. Could it be a draft? The room wasn't exactly airtight. I held my breath, creeping silently in the direction of the sound.

It was one of the rooms no one had opened since we arrived. Giving one last look to make sure no one saw me, I pressed my ear to the door. Had more girls arrived? It had to be the middle of the night. No one else would be up at this hour, would they?

Cressida. She hadn't returned. Maybe the noise was her. Or maybe it was Cytherea's emissary here to give me the weapon I needed. Either way, I had to see who was in that room. I didn't like the idea of Cressida spending time with Eros this late. And if the weapon waited for me just on the other side of this door...

I placed my palm on the cool handle, pressing gently.

Another small noise. I froze, heart thundering.

What was I so afraid of? After another moment, I pushed the handle down again. Unlocked. I eased the door open a fraction.

Once air emerged from the other room, it carried with it more sounds. The thick barrier had muffled most of the noises, furtive and insistent. The glow of a single lantern washed the space with enough light to see two figures sprawled on the ground, one on top of the other. Their clothes were halfway off, breathless kisses, strangled moans...

I startled and made to close the door again when Cressida noticed me first. Foggy with lust, Zepherin took longer to register that Cressida had stopped kissing him, stopped clutching at his clothes.

I could barely register what I was seeing. Didn't Cressida hate Zepherin? And wasn't Zepherin embarrassed by sex?

But she had called him Z. And that fascinated look on his face as she was telling him off...

"Psyche." Cressida's swollen lips parted and her eyes wide with panic.

As though the word had broken a spell, Zepherin scrambled off her, shirt open as he sat back to stare at me, revealing unexpectedly gorgeous abs. A hard erection tented his pants. Both of them were wildly out of breath.

"I'm sorry," I mumbled, retreating.

"Wait!" Zepherin this time.

I paused with my fingers gripping the edge of the door.

"You can't... say anything about this. You can't tell him."

I didn't point out that I wasn't allowed to see Eros unless Zepherin led me to him blindfolded. There was no easy way to tell Eros about this even if I wanted to. And I never would. I wouldn't get Cressida in trouble.

"Please, Psyche," my friend put in.

Then it struck me. Zepherin would owe me a big favor after this—if he didn't recommend I be thrown out...

"How long has this been going on?" I asked.

"Just tonight," Cressida answered quickly.

I hadn't spotted the signs of attraction between them, but perhaps I should have. They both looked up at me like children caught stealing.

"I won't say anything, if you tell Him he should choose me. Then we can all have someone." I gave a faint smile, but my gaze was hard as I looked at Zepherin.

Even in the dim light, all his visible skin looked flushed. From the kiss or fear, I wasn't sure. Probably all three. He blinked a few times, still shaking off the haze.

"Do you agree?" I persisted.

He glanced at Cressida, who nodded after shooting a thankful look at me. She wanted nothing to do with the monster of the mountain. It was nice to see Cressida with someone she wanted more. If Zepherin did as I asked, this could end up better than I'd planned.

"I will," he said, finally.

I beamed. I didn't know how much weight Zepherin's recommendation would hold, but it definitely couldn't hurt my chances. With this added assurance, I was a frontrunner. I had to be.

"Don't be loud," I said as I closed them in the room again, alone.

When I turned around after closing the door, I sucked in a gasp. A figure stood behind me in the dim common area. It was huge—taller than Zepherin, who stood above the human women by a head—and covered head to toe in a brown cloak. The deep hood didn't betray a hint of the being's features, except for a few golden hairs peeking out over one shoulder. It was misshapen, hunchbacked, but stood with ease.

There was a hiss of air, a stiffening of shoulders, and it was gone.

I pressed my hand to my chest as I caught my breath. What was that? *Who* was that?

Once air returned to my lungs, the answer was obvious.

Eros.

But why had he come here if he was clearly terrified to get close to anyone? In his room, he hadn't touched me once. Arriving in the center of our shared space had been a risk, even if he was covered up by that cloak. Those golden hairs... People said he had long, golden hair, but the body seemed to belong to something out of a nightmare, not a wet dream.

My heart still wouldn't slow after the shock. Waves of it continued to hit me, images of men appearing out of darkness. He could appear in my room, in any of our rooms, and no one would know. My eyes darted around the space again, but he was definitely gone.

Slowly, I forced myself to move forward. Near where Eros had stood was a light-colored square. In the gloom, I couldn't make it out.

Swallowing the memories that kept trying to freeze my limbs, I stepped toward it, bent, and picked it up. Would he return to collect this?

That would be good, I reminded myself. If he returned in person, I could seduce him or kill him more easily. But it was difficult to get my soul to believe it when I was weaponless and buzzing with residual terror.

Happily, he didn't appear. I squinted at the object in my hand. Folded parchments. No divine seal. I turned them over in my hand.

From the room next door, soft moans emerged. I'd told them to be quiet. At least Cressida and Zepherin hadn't made noise while Eros was here. I returned to my room where it would be quieter and I could investigate with more light.

Candle lit, I settled down on the side of the bed, picking up the first parchment in the stack. On one side, in florid handwriting, read the word *Psyche*.

My brows ticked downward. Was this really for me, or had Eros dropped it by mistake? I held my breath for a few heart-beats, listening, but the demi-god didn't appear. Carefully, I unfolded the paper—it was addressed to me, after all—and read.

Psyche, I'm sorry for making you leave my chambers so soon...

Despite myself, I chuckled at Eros' apology. I'd aroused him. *Good.* I read on.

...It torments me that you might flee when you know the truth.

I pursed my lips. I did know the truth, and I had no intention of fleeing. His unexpected presence had startled me, that was all. Maybe Eros actually was hideous and dreadful under that cloak, not beautiful as everyone supposed. He did seem a bit obsessed with the question of his appearance. It didn't matter to me. He could be a half-snake monster and I'd still wed him for a chance to be free and earn peace with Cytherea.

I flipped through the rest of the papers. There was one for each of us. I burned to know what he'd written to the other women, but the letters were sealed. In the morning, I'd pass them out and ask what each one said.

Then I realized he expected a response. I couldn't remember the last time I'd written anything. I could read, but would my writing look like a child's? I barely had more practice than one. Besides, I didn't own a pen.

I jumped to Cressida's side of the room but still couldn't find a pen and paper. Zepherin would bring some if I asked, but he was a little busy. I'd reply in the morning. In the meantime, I'd mull over my response. Part of me wanted to call him out for not addressing the Eros-suna but instead fixating on his own appearance.

Well, I already knew Eros was shallow.

As I fell asleep, I imagined him touching himself to memories of me.

❧ 16 ❧

PSYCHE

To Him.

I do not plan to flee. Remember, beautiful things can be toxic and ugly things can be wonderful. Looks aren't everything, and I like you.

Psyche.

It took me much longer than I expected to craft a reply to Eros' letter. (I'd wanted to use the word *poison* instead of *toxic* but I couldn't spell it.) If I revealed that I knew he was attractive—at least in reputation—then he'd suspect I knew his true identity. More than he suspected it now, anyway. If I called him hideous, I doubted that would win me favor with the vain demi-god. Hopefully this would be enough to secure his choice. He wasn't basing it on much, after all. A little flattery, a little seduction...

My head went woozy for a moment. I was so close to the end. Cytherea would catch wind of the situation and provide me with the knife before the marriage, right? I wished I could contact her, just once.

Setting my jaw, I folded the note and wrote *Him* on the top as nicely as I could. Out in the main area, I found Zepherin easily. He was much taller than any of the women, studiously avoiding Cressida, who stood on the opposite side of the room.

"Can you bring this to... Him for me?" I asked, thrusting it into his hand.

He looked down as if he'd been thinking of something else and was surprised to find me standing there. Just like when I'd asked him for pen and paper, his cheeks flushed a little as he looked at me and his pupils widened. Whether it was because of what I'd caught him doing last night or because of what he'd seen me do in Eros' chamber, I wasn't sure.

"Yes, sure," he muttered.

I lowered my voice. "Is everything all right between you and—?"

He gestured so suddenly I thought he'd clasp a hand over my mouth, but he held back, eyes darting wildly. "No. Yes!" His answers came out in fierce whispers. Suddenly puzzled, he looked more closely at the letter I'd passed him. A new expression sent chills down my spine. He stood perfectly still now, almost violently so as he peered down at me through narrowed lids. "You didn't...?" He held up the note.

"No!" I exclaimed. "You can read it if you like." I fixed him with a look that I hoped said that I wished him and Cressida no harm.

His stone face didn't thaw. My throat constricted. Zepherin was a demi-god too, and he finally showed it. Feminine wiles took him out of his depth, but when it came to threats to his security or the security of those he wanted to protect, he could be a terrifying force. His position as one of Eros' favorites made more sense.

"Really," I urged. "Read it."

With measured breaths, he unfolded the paper and let his gaze roam over the words. When he did, his hard-set eyes and sharp jawline finally relaxed. His eyes flicked back to meet mine.

"If he picks me..." I began, barely a whisper, but he understood my question. *What will you and Cressida do?*

"I don't know." His attention finally locked onto Cressida, talking to Xanthi across the room. There was no searching. He'd known exactly where she was the whole time.

When his gaze landed on her, she met his eyes. From where I stood, I felt their secret like something tangible connecting them. Then Cressida's focus lowered to me.

When I held up her letter, she broke off her conversation she ushered Xanthi over too. Zepherin drifted away from my side as they approached.

"What's that?" Cressida took the parchment addressed to her. I hadn't heard her return last night, so I hadn't had the chance to give it to her until now.

"It's a letter from Him. You have one too, Xanthi. Everyone does." I handed them out as the women realized what was happening.

"Did you already read yours, Psyche?" Cressida asked. "How did you get them all first?" Her frown told me she was thinking of Zepherin, who usually handled this kind of thing.

"I found them in the common room."

Xanthi's eyes traced back and forth over the page. After a few seconds, I could tell her letter was longer than mine. My heart tightened at the realization. Did Eros want her more than he wanted me?

I respected secrets. I really did. But I burned to know what was in their letters.

When Cressida gave a half-smile as she read her own, I cracked. "What did he say?"

"You can read it," she offered, handing it back to me.

Cressida,

There's little I admire more than a rebel. You won't simply fall at my feet and that's all right. I don't want someone to do that. I prefer people who question things, people who understand their own worth and respect the worth of others. I sense that protecting that worth has been a fight.

When I looked at you—I'm sorry you could not look at me—I saw you were coiled tight. Whether it's with me or others, I hope you find someone to uncoil you. You are beautiful and fierce, Cressida.

I have a question. Do you think you could love me, as things stand now?

Him

My breath shallowed. It was a beautiful letter that struck to the heart of Cressida's character. I wished I could have written it. Although in a different way, it was just as intimate as mine.

Something bitter rested on the back of my tongue. I didn't want to consider what it meant. When I looked at Cressida again, she shook her head. No, she couldn't love him.

That was some consolation, at least. If I'd read him right, that would disqualify her from becoming Eros's bride. But I'd been wrong about a few things. I had thought he might like me most, but now doubt wormed in.

"He really is sweet," Stantina said softly from behind me.

All four girls surrounded me, reading their letters, and I felt the urge to escape. My reply to Eros seemed woefully inadequate now. What did I have to offer except my sexuality? By reputation, he valued that, but here he showed more sides to himself. He was more than just the demi-god of lust. He wanted more than lust in a relationship after all.

My voice sounded too scratchy when I asked Stantina if she'd tell us what she meant.

"Oh," she said, "he just tried to make me laugh so I wouldn't be so nervous." She bit her lip. "And he promised he'd bring all the berries and cream I want." With a shrug both uncomfortable and pleased, she turned back to read the letter again.

Was everyone starting to fall for Eros? All it took was a personal letter to turn all the fear and animosity to soft consideration of his offer?

My ribcage closed, pressing my insides too small. I was upset that I might not win the bridal contest, that was all.

It wasn't that I liked him more with every interaction we had, or that his letters warmed a deep place inside me, or that the last part of my own letter to Eros might be true. Because I didn't like him. I hated him.

I hated him for stealing Cytherea's worship and allowing his Eros-suna to destroy Card. I hated him for demanding women for his bride. I hated him because he stood in the way of my happy ending near the goddess I admired.

Sure, I lusted after him a little, but I was in the business of pleasure. I looked for it wherever I could. Lust didn't equal love. My life had proven that one hundred times over.

I told myself to breathe as I rotated, looking at the women all re-reading their letters while their features softened. It was good that they felt seen and cared about.

A few paces away, Zepherin was trying to pretend he wasn't staring at Cressida, but the worried lines on his forehead betrayed him. They mirrored the way I felt.

Jealous.

I tried to snap out of my spiral. I did not love Eros. I didn't even like him.

Except...

No matter where I looked, despite excessive precautions like the blindfolds, I saw evidence of someone who cared fiercely for all living things, who struggled through his own crippling fear to call out the good in others. That was more than mindless lust. Paired with it, though... My stomach flipped and heat throbbed in my core.

I thought of his letter. My mission hadn't changed. I still had to assassinate him at the end of this, one way or another, but I had to admit something to myself.

I didn't want to anymore.

More revelations scratched beneath the surface, but I wouldn't let them out. I couldn't afford more of the truth. Not when we were both trapped with no other way out.

❦ 17 ❦

EROS

I smiled down at the letter in my hand. I'd already memorized the words, but I couldn't hep running my eyes over them one more time.

Her simple response had been enough to confirm my hope. Psyche liked me. She wanted me. And I wanted her. Gods, how I wanted her. The faintest thought of her set my blood and mind on fire.

"I'm choosing Psyche," I said on an exhale, not looking up from the letter. "Send the rest home." Relief lapped against me. A decision at last, and one I was excited about. When was the last time I'd felt genuine hope?

When no prompt response came, I glanced up. Standing at attention near the door, Zepherin blanched. "But the rest..." he finally sputtered. "Are you sure she's the best choice?" He clamped his mouth shut, jaw flexing.

My lieutenant's heart raced. He wasn't telling me something. I gave my wings a shake and squinted at him.

"Psyche is the only one who replied to my letter," I

answered. "She's the only one who said she wanted me. I won't marry someone against their will."

Another jaw flex at that. I didn't appreciate the criticism.

It didn't help that nerves fluttered in my stomach. Given the short timeframe I had to make this huge decision, Psyche offered the best chance of happiness and success, but marriage was still an enormous commitment—one I had never planned to make with one person.

"Why do you have to choose so quickly?" Zepherin asked.

"The eclipse," I said. If Cytherea found out there was a time limit to ending my life, I and anyone defending me would face a barrage of attacks unlike anything I'd suffered so far. This fortress would be no barrier against her wrath. "Is there a reason I should wait?"

His heartbeat kicked up even more. "There are some good candidates there. What about Cybel?"

If I wasn't suspicious before, I was now. Suspicious of what exactly, I didn't know. "I like Cybel. I wish I had more time to spend with each of them. I wish they didn't have to wear blindfolds whenever we talked. I wish you didn't have to stand that far away from me every time we spoke." Blood rushed to my cheeks. "I wish a lot of things, but I don't have the luxury of them. Is there something wrong with Psyche that I shouldn't choose her?"

Surely Zepherin wasn't holding her display in my bedroom against her somehow?

At the thought, I stepped on his reply. "I like her, Zeph. I like her a lot. She's smart and sexy and brave. I think she'll make a good partner." That I wanted to listen to her almost as much as I wanted to bed her was an excellent sign. I glanced at the bed that still held her delicious scent. The memory of it sent an ache to my chest and made my length stiffen. I wanted to fall into reveries of what I would do to her, but I wrenched myself out to finish what I needed to say. "And she's the only one who wants me too. It's done. It's her."

"Are you sure she doesn't *know*?"

I frowned. A familiar embrace, like freezing wind, enveloped me in fear. Of course it had occurred to me, but if I waited for absolute certainty, I'd never take a step forward. I'd spent too many years frozen in fear. "Have you heard her say anything?" I asked, my voice dangerous and brittle at once.

"No." But his answer held no conviction.

With Cytherea's reach, she *could* have corrupted Psyche. I hated the thought. Gazing back at that look Zepherin was giving me, I struggled to shake off the idea as mere paranoia. This felt too similar to Pothos, who waited until I was helpless with passion before attacking me.

Helpless with passion. I'd give anything to experience that same helplessness with Psyche, and feel safe. I couldn't remember wanting anyone as much as I wanted her. I wanted to trace the curve of her tempting lips, to peel away her clothes, to ride her until we both knew nothing but the pulsing friction of our bodies. If I talked to Psyche again, I wouldn't be able to hold back. All my careful self-denial would crumble into dust and the chaos within would roar free. Her sensuality and intelligence made it inevitable. I had no weapons to withstand her. Thank the gods she gave me more reasons to choose her.

"What is it then?" I snapped as Zepherin continued giving me that dubious look. "Do you suspect her of something?"

"No, that's not what I meant," he said quickly. "I just want to make sure you had enough time to make a good decision. That's it."

"Then send the rest home. And prepare for the marriage ceremony. Olitor can assist you."

As I predicted, Zepherin's breath shallowed at Olitor's name, his heart pounding an uneven rhythm. "Will you... need me as often after we deliver them back to their families?"

The question stung. Did Zepherin want to leave? I almost laughed at myself. He'd wanted to leave ever since I demanded he serve as my lieutenant in hiding. But, over the years, I couldn't help letting him into my heart. I had no one else to lean on, and he'd served me faithfully. The goddess wouldn't hunt him down if he left... I didn't think. So why shouldn't he be free?

I tried to swallow the lump in my throat. "No. Not as often." *Or at all*. But I couldn't say the words out loud. Instead, I turned to a topic that didn't make me sad. "You'll have plenty of free time to dally with whoever you want."

Zepherin blanched. "I didn't... I'm not..."

"It's fine," I said, waving a dismissive hand and allowing a sly smile to curl my lips. "I like seeing you together."

"You... do?"

"My time will come soon enough. When you tell Psyche and arrange the marriage." I didn't want a big ceremony, just enough to make it official so Lox would help me. The quicker the better, so I could let Psyche be free to see and touch me.

"So... can she stay?"

I stared. What was he talking about? "Psyche will stay," I said slowly. "We're marrying."

"No. Cressida."

His answer left me dumbfounded. "Cressida?" I liked Cressida but had no plans for a harem. "Only Psyche's staying."

"But you said..."

Finally, the truth dawned. Zepherin wasn't attracted to Olitor, but to Cressida. One of my potential brides.

"Did you sleep with her?" I asked in a voice like ice.

Blood drained from Zepherin's face. I hated that he feared me, but I hated what he did even more. "Yes, my lord."

What if I had chosen Cressida? I had considered it. What would he have done? Would they have carried on an affair behind my back?

All my days alone, wings bound, yearning for companionship I couldn't have, flooded back in a storm of anger. It seized my throat like a sob. In the days when I trusted no one, Zepherin had been my closest friend. That wasn't saying much, since he didn't stand close to me and I still kept secrets. But I depended on him. I talked to him, gave him access to my private room.

It hadn't taken another manipulation by Cytherea to create this betrayal. I longed with lung-deep passion for closeness, yet Zepherin had done something that could have undermined even this attempt.

The walls closed more tightly around my wings. I tucked them in to protect them from the contracting room that threatened to squeeze out my breath. *Never safe, never safe, never safe...*

My gaze flashed to the bow and arrows hung on the wall. I couldn't punish Zepherin even if I wanted to. I'd let myself die first. That knowledge pressed like a bruise against his disloyalty.

"Get out and go tell Psyche," I growled, chest heaving as I tried and failed to steady myself. Chaos and panic swirled like darkness around me. I couldn't utter another syllable—not about sending away the rest of the women or reminding him to keep my secret from Cytherea or else I'd... I didn't know.

Zepherin ran to obey.

I stood in the center of my bedroom, wings tucked and eyes stinging.

I'd thought that announcing this decision would feel joyous. Now, even the thought of being alone with Psyche put me on edge.

I realized I still held Psyche's note in one hand. I'd crushed it. Flattening it out again took every careful nerve. I set it down, skin zinging.

Unable to bear the interior pressure building from Zepherin's betrayal, I yelled in frustration and shoved a plant to the ground. Its pot shattered. The weight and the crash were satisfying, but seeing the thing sprawled like that, roots exposed and leaves askew, sent a fresh wave of shame over me.

Not even Psyche in all her brilliance could free me from the fear that kept me chained.

The five of us let out tiny gasps. Lines spidered from Zepherin's bright eyes as he forced a smile after his announcement.

I'd done it. Relief left me lightheaded. Since I'd arrived, I hoped I was a frontrunner, but the possibility that Eros could choose someone other than me had hung over my head like a blade about to fall.

Now it was official. Eros chose me.

Unwelcome warmth tugged at my middle. This felt different from being chosen as a sexual companion in the temple or being picked off the street. It felt like *more* somehow. Before, I was a beautiful thing to be used. Now, with Eros —it was foolish even to think—I felt cared about. In a small but poignant way, I felt seen. Seen, and still chosen.

Beside me, Cressida pressed her lips together so hard they almost disappeared. She stared hard at Zepherin. Elation at my victory fizzed away. Winning felt so good it made me selfish. What would this announcement mean for everyone else?

"The marriage ceremony will take place tomorrow," Zepherin continued.

So fast. I reeled. For some reason, the marriage aspect of my mission had always been secondary in my thoughts. To me, the important parts were to win his affection, get Eros alone, and finish the job—which I'd all but forgotten about for a moment. I'd finished the first task, but to reach the second, I had to marry a monster. Because Eros was a monster, no matter how kindly he spoke to stolen women.

Zepherin didn't look back at Cressida. His next words were mechanical, soldier-like. "The rest of you will be escorted home."

As if by magic, the handsome gardener appeared, just like the time he'd taken Gia away. I stiffened. Cressida was my only friend here. If she left, I'd truly be alone. And what would Zepherin do once she left? How serious was their fling?

"Wait! I'd... I..." The voice was mine. I felt as surprised as the others, who all swiveled their attention to me in astonishment. My mouth felt gummy, but I had to say something now. "I would like the other women to help me get ready for the wedding first."

The boyish, unsure version of Zepherin returned. Astonishment painted his striking features. His gaze shifted quickly to Cressida then to all the others as he considered my request. Finally, he regarded me. "I don't see why not." A hint of defiance laced his response, though not defiance against me.

I smiled. "Then... can you explain the ceremony to me?"

WE RETURNED TO THE POOL WHERE WE HAD BATHED WHEN we'd first arrived. Zepherin provided soaps and oils. I didn't need four helpers to smooth lotions into my skin or scrub my hair with tonics that smelled like pomegranate and vanilla, but one person, at least, seemed grateful for my request to have all the women help.

Cressida chewed her lip, staying behind as the other three went to replenish supplies. "What do I do?" she asked so quietly I couldn't be sure I'd heard her.

"I don't know," I admitted. "I think he's serious about sending you home instead of... you know..."

She nodded. Even Stantina didn't think Eros executed the dismissed girls anymore, not after the letters. Cressida sighed. "I needed more time to think." It was as good as a thank you.

I placed a wet hand on her bare shoulder.

"What about you?" she continued. "Are you...?"

Will I be all right?

It was my turn to nod. "I will be. I get to marry the monster of the mountain."

Cressida laughed joylessly.

I lowered my voice so the returning women wouldn't catch my next words. "I hear demi-gods can fuck you unconscious."

Cressida squeaked, blushing as she smacked my arm. I grinned.

As the others returned, a memory returned with them.

Zepherin had said that even on the wedding night, Eros' bride would have to consent not to see his face. And to be bound. An... interesting prospect. If it weren't with my enemy, I'd be happy to try it. I didn't fear bondage—such things were a matter of conversation among the temple courtesans—but to not be able to touch Eros while I gave him free rein to touch me...?

I didn't relish the thought. At what point would he let me see him, or at least free me to feel my way toward him? I didn't want to be trapped as a blind bride. And I wouldn't be. I'd find some way to sneak into his chambers if I had to. As soon as I had Cytherea's knife, I'd retrace the steps I'd memorized to his bedroom, assuming he wouldn't let me sleep beside him, and strike him in the heart.

When I brought my attention back to the warm water and the sensation of the comb pulling through my hair, Cressida was gone.

"Did you see where Cressida went?" I asked.

"I think she needed to step out," Xanthi answered, rubbing oil over each of my fingers. The excess drops gathered on top of the water.

I scanned the cave-like space. No Cressida.

My heart jolted. I double-checked the water's edge. No Zepherin either.

My chest grew tighter. They couldn't have... run? Running put them in danger. It would alert Eros that the two of them were together. The unbidden image of the dead man speared through by a massive arrow clogged my thoughts. Rumor had it that the monster of the mountain had done that. Could Eros shoot the lovers if he sensed betrayal?

All the deathless were known to be mercurial, temperamental. Eros might be angry enough to attack. I silently prayed to the goddess that they would survive.

Hopefully, my expression hid my fear, but hands were on me and my breathing had grown shaky. Xanthi gave me a look dark with curiosity.

I didn't address her, just bit down on my lower lip to steady myself.

Good thing Eros had something to distract him from any potential violence—our impending wedding.

By the time we got out of the pool, the other women had noticed the absence too. No sign of Cressida or Zepherin had reemerged. I had no doubt. The couple had fled.

And Zepherin hadn't even told me what to expect at the ceremony.

Uncertainty shifted the ground beneath my feet as I wrapped myself in a robe to return to our quarters. I didn't know what else to do. I almost laughed at the absurdity and tried not to feel ashamed about how unsteady I was, how part of me feared what I might do next.

Everything was spiraling and I did my best to hang on. Just beneath my skin, violence struggled for an outlet. Danger meant I had to defend myself, right? And right now, standing in that robe, I felt more vulnerable than I ever had. Men fucking me in the temple hadn't made me feel this vulnerable. Surviving on the streets only approximated this feeling. At least then I had a label.

Courtesan.

Survivor.

Murderer.

Now, with Cressida gone and a marriage to Eros impending, pieces of me scattered until nothing but the core of the girl was left, and I didn't know who that was. Did I love Eros or hate him? Who would I be once this job was done? A good worshipper? For some reason, that sounded hollow right now.

I was a bundle of longings. For a second, I allowed myself to feel, but I didn't know words for the emotion that rose up, only that it was strong.

I clutched the robe in shaking fists.

"Are you okay, Psyche?" Stantina asked, giving me a hesitant hug around the shoulders.

"I'm fine," I answered quickly. "I'm just a little concerned about..." I glanced pointedly at my room, and everyone understood.

"They must have taken Cressida back first," Xanthi reasoned.

I nodded absently.

After a few more minutes, I was left to return to my room —to *our* room—alone.

Enough feeling sorry for myself. No more confusion. I knew some things for sure. Eros or one of his cronies (not Zepherin, I was sure of that) would fetch me for the ceremony tomorrow, whatever that entailed. In the meantime, I needed that knife.

"Cytherea," I whispered aloud. "I did it. I'm marrying Eros tomorrow." I held out my damp, glistening hands. When nothing happened, I closed my eyes. "Please. I need your gift."

Water from my hair dripped on the floor in the answering silence.

"My goddess, I will see Eros alone tomorrow."

Still no response.

How was I supposed to get this dagger? I hadn't seen a single weapon while I'd been here. Zepherin even checked our mouths for dangerous tools. No meal had included a knife.

For a frantic second, I was convinced this had all been a trick. Cytherea laughed to see me wed to an actual monster after I'd desecrated her temple by murdering that man. My heartbeat galloped.

Abandoned, again.

But no. She wanted Eros dead. I would trust her, just as I always had. Somehow, she'd get me that weapon.

For now, I would marry Eros. And then, for the goddess, myself, and now Cressida's safety, I'd kill him.

PSYCHE

I didn't have time to say goodbye before the gardener whisked away the other three women before the wedding. Stripping away the slim companionship they offered left me feeling more naked than I'd been in the pool.

Eros wouldn't harm them, but it was harder to think he wouldn't hunt down Zepherin and Cressida. Eros was a demi-god. Having one of his trusted enforcers run away with his potential bride wouldn't sit well with him.

I took a calming breath and cinched the ribbon round my waist. After he'd disappeared with the women, the gardener returned with a dress for the ceremony. It was simpler than I'd expected. Dove gray silk cascaded from a dipping neckline into a floor-length skirt. A pale pink ribbon crossed in an X to accentuate the chest before wrapping around the waist. Pearl-studded slippers came last. The gardener provided no adorn-ments for my hair or wrists, though he had allowed me to change into the dress alone without searching me. A small comfort.

When I emerged into the large common area, bare now but for us, I turned obediently so he could secure the blindfold.

"Ready?" he asked when he was finished.

It was the first word I'd heard him say aloud. The rich voice sounded familiar, though it took me a moment to place it. Olitor. The second presence during my private time with Eros in his chambers.

My neck heated and gut fluttered with nerves. I couldn't turn back now.

"Yes." But the answer came out a whisper.

"He's waiting for you."

"Olitor." I chanced his name. His guiding hand on my shoulder stilled. "What's the ceremony like?"

Gods were glorious and savage. Tales of these private ceremonies never reached humans except through rumor and legend.

"There won't be many spectators."

His answer did nothing to calm my burgeoning fears.

"Do I have to do anything specific?"

Worrying about details like this felt trivial compared to the magnitude of the task ahead, but I got nervous in the spotlight without an idea of what to do.

Olitor pushed me gently to get me to walk forward. "Make your vow."

"Is it... repeated, or...?" My own breathlessness surprised me.

There was a smile in Olitor's reply. "I believe you can repeat his. I think my lord wants something quick and simple."

Quick and simple. That didn't sound so bad.

Olitor led me out through the antiseptic-smelling hallway past where I knew the path bent toward Eros' bedroom and through a few more passages. Despite my efforts to memorize the way, my distracting thoughts made me miss turns.

Finally, we halted.

"Is this it?" I whispered. The sound echoed.

Olitor didn't answer. Instead, he said, "My lord," and let go of me. I felt suspended in night blackness. How many people were here with me? Where was Eros? What if Cytherea really had abandoned me?

My breath came in short, choppy bursts.

"Psyche." Eros' voice now, very near. Maybe a body length in front of me. My skin responded as if he'd touched me. "Why are you so nervous?" He said it confidentially, but I didn't know how many people could still hear his question.

"I don't like to be the center of attention," I said. Partly true.

A warm chuckle. "I know that's not always true."

It had been easy to ignore Zepherin and Olitor as I spread myself in Eros' bedroom. Besides, I'd done acts like those in the temple. This felt different. A demi-god was marrying me in front of an unknown crowd. They weren't looking *through* me for their own pleasure, but *at* me. Maybe these were monsters too.

My voice dropped to a whisper. "How many are here?" Before, the blindfold hadn't felt as much like a risk. Now, I couldn't be sure exactly where I was or with whom. I couldn't defend myself if—

"Just the two of us and Olitor, and someone to perform the ceremony." His warm tone reassured me. Maybe this room sounded big because Eros didn't want anyone getting close to him. Four people required extra space.

A muffled question came from far away. "Are you ready to begin, my lord?" This time it was a female, diplomatic and confident. None of the women I'd arrived here with.

"A moment," he answered. "Psyche, will you be all right?"

"Yes."

"I... You agree to this? It's all right to say no."

Eros' words soothed me enough to calm. I found my poise again, that mask I wore at the temple. "Absolutely."

He made a noise somewhere between a hum and a groan, effortlessly sexual, and said more loudly, "We're ready to begin."

We. Not *I*. A strange knot tugged at my stomach. For a selfish bastard, Eros consistently didn't act the part.

"This alliance is blessed by the gods," the woman began. "Together you will remain until death claims you."

I held my breath. Would she say Eros' name and confirm his identity?

No, it turned out. Her speech was short. No talk of love, but alliances. Vows that bound us together. Formal and brief.

Olitor had been right. Eros wanted this over quickly. For one of the first times, I considered why. But before I could come up with an answer, the woman announced, "You have until tomorrow to consummate the marriage."

We hadn't touched throughout the ceremony. I couldn't even see. Yet now I was bound to him for eternity, as the vows said, or until death claimed one of us.

"Will now do?" Eros asked a little roughly.

My mouth dried. Now, finally, I'd be alone with Eros. "Yes. Now."

"Olitor."

Fingers grasped my shoulder gently and led me from the room.

Now, I prayed. But no blade materialized. Sweat beaded on my neck as footsteps took me farther from my target, my husband.

❧ 20 ❧

EROS

*F*uck.

Psyche had been bound spread eagle, with restraints at her wrists and ankles and a blindfold over her eyes. The bonds didn't look too tight, but the image pierced my conscience.

Zepherin told them about this and she still said yes. Hadn't he? He'd deceived me about other things regarding the women. I shoved the thought away. Now wasn't the time for thinking, but for doing.

My skipping mind barely formed the next important question. *Could Psyche have denied me, though?*

My skin zinged hot with static at the sight of her naked body. There. In my room. For me.

I'd make sure she was willing, even though I wanted to bolt forward and mold my body to hers. Right now.

"I'm here, Psyche," I croaked, already getting traitorously hard.

"Come closer, then." Even bound, her confidence exceeded mine.

The pit of my stomach flipped as I approached. I could feel her heartbeat. It wasn't thundering as quickly as mine, but anticipation rang through her veins as well.

I lapped up every detail of her form—her silky black hair, the smooth skin of her throat, the swell of her breasts to perfect tips. Her warm body drew me irresistibly forward.

Arm's length. I hadn't crossed this threshold willingly in half a century. Everything in me longed to rush in, to touch, but I had to take this carefully.

A sensuous curve of Psyche's mouth suggested she saw bondage as more of a game than a threat. That was good. That was very good. My breathing shallowed.

I undid the knot at my throat in one motion and unclipped the strap holding down my wings. I'd worn my disguise even through the ceremony. Irena and Olitor knew who I was, but I couldn't let down my guard so completely.

Releasing myself only increased my desire. The stretching of my wings registered all the way down my back to my hips.

I pulled off my gloves finger by finger, savoring the anticipation.

Husky with dryness, I said, "I have to check your mouth."

Obediently, she opened for me. Wet and waiting.

I stepped forward, the heat from our bodies mingling in the space between us. She was utterly gorgeous, small, but with curves I could get lost in. Everything she did and said captivated me. And what had I done? I'd treated her as a slave.

Not tonight. Tonight, I would make her feel like the queen she was, even though I couldn't rip off her bonds yet.

I didn't fold the gloves. I tossed them carelessly on the nearby bed before raising two fingers toward her skin. Closer. Years of cultivated paranoia melted like wax in the flame of desire.

I grazed her bare shoulder. The light touch set my arm ablaze. Her skin soft against the pads of my fingertips... It sent memories flashing back. Passionate nights. The height of my reign in my corner of the kingdom.

Her skin was home.

Trailing upward, I traced her strong jaw down to her chin, every burning line a path to be explored. I didn't remember skin feeling so good, so alive. Her pulse quickened just a little, solidifying my resolve to discover exactly how to draw pleasure out of her. How could I make her heart flutter with desperation, to make her beg for more?

My fingers slipped over the ridge of her bottom lip and into her warm mouth. Blood pumped in my core. Slowly, I searched inside, slicking under her tongue, then back out. She caught the tip of my longest finger between her lips before we broke contact.

She wanted this. Wanted me.

The fabric of my trousers stretched painfully against my growing erection.

"Now," I said, the syllable a breathy growl, "underneath." My chest heaved until I was almost lightheaded. It wasn't that I doubted my prowess, but I hadn't been able to do this in so long. And now to do it with Psyche, who impressed me in every way. Relief sucked me down like an undertow.

My wet fingers drew on her collarbone where a pink flush was growing. I craved more contact, more skin, but I had to complete my checks first. The knowledge made me rush, skipping with a frustrated breath over her breasts, her ribs, her stomach, to land at the apex of her thighs. She was warm, a little swollen, but not wet yet. Still, the slide of her folds as I opened her with my two fingers before plunging inside...

Her head fell back with a cry. "Ah, yes!"

I straightened and took the back of her head gently but firmly in my free hand. Her breath feathered against my face. We were so close. I would only have to lean forward to press her mouth to mine.

"No pretending. Don't pretend with me." I knew a moment of true ecstasy from a fake one. The entire body flushed and sheened with sweat, muscles contracted and released, the sound would have ragged edges. No, I hadn't yet awakened my wife.

But I would.

"Promise," I said, bringing my face even closer.

She exhaled through parted lips. "Are you sure?" The question was baldly honest, not even teasing. She'd been with men before.

I smiled. She'd never been with me. "Yes. Very sure. Don't make a sound unless you must."

Finally, her skin began to warm. I sensed the blood churning faster in her veins. "But I could make you feel like a god every time," she said.

The slosh of blood in my ears roared like the ocean tide. "You don't have to do that. It's my responsibility to..."

But she was breathing heavily. My hand still between her legs felt the moment she opened wider, loosening. She whimpered in half-formed groans. I could hardly contain myself.

Her body and her noises were pure sex. Her sounds crested higher, her head falling against my hand, back arching. Her stomach touched mine for one ember-glowing second. Her cries grew louder, wilder, insisting, barely articulate.

Fascinated, I kept my invasive hand inside her as she writhed, but gave her no more motivation to orgasm.

"Oh, yes! Ah... harder... oh, gods!" A broken scream ended her demonstration.

Her head straightened. If she'd been able to see, she would have leveled a knowing look at me.

I swallowed against a parched throat. "No pretending," I repeated, though she'd just given the most impressive performance I'd ever witnessed. Her temperature had risen slightly. She'd even gotten wetter. I removed my fingers from between her legs, dragging up through the crease.

To calm myself down, I bent to touch my forehead to hers. Something animalistically comforting welled up in me at the gesture.

Contact at last. Not only was I harder than I'd ever been in my life, but the sensation of closeness brought a swell of emotion. No matter what Zepherin had implied, Psyche made me feel safe.

"I'm sorry it has to be like this," I said, stroking her cheek. "I promise it isn't forever. Do you trust me?"

"I trust you."

But I'd just seen how well she could lie. My cock believed every bit of it.

"I won't take you until you ask me to," I promised.

A shallowing of breath. Now I was getting somewhere. I glanced down. Her nipples had become hard points.

"That's it," I murmured, bringing one hand down to cup her breast. The soft weight of her, the center like a pebble in my palm... "My gods." I touched my forehead to hers again, kneading her. "You're perfect." And it was true. Even among my other consorts, I'd never felt this much anticipation.

It was more than the decades I'd waited. It was Psyche herself, stealing my breath with her beauty and strength.

She tilted her head against mine, asking for my lips. With a groan, I let myself answer, pressing my mouth to hers. Her kiss tasted like fire, like some fantastical dessert I could eat until I suffocated. My mind formed nothing but desperate curses and feral need. She moved with such grace and urgency against me, mouth open, tongue tasting our sensual feast.

My body pushed flush against hers. The expanse of skin at my belly only enflamed me more. I wanted her arms around me, her eyes looking into mine.

Soon. Soon I would remove all restraints and fear.

Still kissing, I removed my trousers at last, freeing the thick, hard cock. I stretched out my wings for good measure, as far as they would go, and a smile curled my mouth.

Breaking the kiss, I traveled to her uplifted arms, touching my lips to the underside of them. I checked her pulse. Good, but I could do better.

Next her neck. Just kisses, tastes, memorizing her salty-sweet flavor. Not much change in her pulse when I did that. Unusual.

I ran feather-light hands over her sides down to her hips, relishing the feel of her. Her lack of a strong response caught me off guard. Was it because she couldn't see me? Again, I wanted to yank off the blindfold. But that would be foolish until the deal with Lox was done. Curse it.

Did she not want me like I thought she did?

I nuzzled her neck, rumbling into her ear. "Tonight is about you, love. Teach me your body."

A shiver. I drew in a deep breath of her musky scent and smirked. If she wanted me to talk, to praise her, I could do that.

"Do you want me to rub you, like this?" I held her between her legs and felt for that sweet point with my thumb, the same point I'd seen her touch in front of me.

Her chest trembled with an intaken breath.

"Yes?" I pushed back and forth. She grew wetter. "What if I do this?" My mouth closed over her breast. After one lick, I sucked hard. "Oh, these breasts... Do you like this?"

"Yes," she breathed, and I believed her.

I did it again with the other side, still stroking her. Between her breasts was a small mark, maybe a scar. "What's this?" I gave it a kiss.

Her breath caught. Either she liked that very much or she was nervous. Psyche didn't seem the type to get nervous. I kissed her again, this time lingeringly, feeling the heat of her breasts on either side of my face.

"I love the taste of you," I said low in my throat. It was an understatement. "Let me taste you here."

I moved my thumb aside and kneeled to plunge my face between her legs, sucking hard as I'd done on her nipples. Her thighs trembled. Her heady sweetness nearly drove me mad. The chaos inside roared to come out. I nipped and licked and sucked, drinking her in.

Taking handfuls of her ass, I lifted her so she sat backward on my shoulders, legs dangling without adding tension to the bonds at her wrists. Her bare feet teased the base of my wings. A shuddering groan ripped out of me. In the corner of my eye, my pinions curled forward in response to her touch. My whole body coiled, waiting for release, even as I enjoyed this delicious moment.

"Keep doing that," I instructed.

She brushed her toes along the top of my wing. When I kissed her hard in thanks, her back flexed backward above my hands.

"You like it when I feast on you, my delicious wife?"

I could tell her silence now was because she was trying to hold in her cries.

"Mmm." I growled against her pussy. Goosebumps spread across her inner thigh. I chased them with kisses.

My wings had contracted so far with arousal that they wrapped almost entirely around us, a white barrier from the rest of the world, making the light shadowy.

I matched the rhythm of my tongue to the rhythm of her rubbing foot. "Yes," I muttered in a gasp. I was drowning and didn't want to breathe.

Her breathing came in labored pants too. I was a new player of her instrument, but I had already learned a few chords.

"How can I make our wedding night better, my love? How can I adore you?"

"Make me come," she demanded. "I want you inside me."

21

PSYCHE

Eros told me not to pretend. I wasn't pretending. Wetness dripped down the inside of my legs as he eased me off his shoulders. His words and fingers had been so gentle, not snatching what he wanted, but coaxing pleasure from me. I felt like the goddess herself when he touched me, whispering hoarse words of adoration. It didn't matter that I was bound and blind. The care he took made each sensation sweeter and more surprising.

The lightest touch of wings grazed my back. I shivered.

"Take me. Get inside me," I said. My core was molten and pulsing hard.

"Psyche." My name was a breathless plea. He anchored his hands on my hips and I felt him nudge my entrance.

Hot blood flushed my cheeks. He was... big.

Even with my experience in the temple, he felt enormous, big enough to fill me until I turned inside out.

With a grunt, he eased the tip inside. My inner muscles arranged to make room for him as he pushed in further.

Despite how slick I was, how ready, I hadn't expected him to feel like this—expanding my walls, filling me to bursting.

I made a straining noise against Eros's neck. His hand came up immediately to caress my back. "You're doing good. You can do it. You can take all of me."

With a small roll of his hips, he went deeper. Even the pain left me wanting more. I was an ache, and he knew how to fill it.

"More," I said, flexing against him, trying to make room.

His noise was feral. He pushed hard. There was even more of him. Long and thick. How much more? Maybe he was half-snake after all. With a groan and another thrust, he was balls deep inside me.

"You feel…" But what I felt like he couldn't say. Those two erotic syllables told me everything. He kissed my cheek.

I couldn't speak. I just bucked against him. The motion sent him into a rhythm.

Every movement continued the adoration he'd professed at the beginning. He was buried inside me so deeply that each small pulse rocked my entire body. It felt like he opened new regions, dark and rich and secret. Dreams of exceeding Cytherea herself. Dreams of being loved instead of used.

My next request came out piecemeal. "More… Wings…." I wasn't even sure what I meant, but I knew I wanted the feeling of feathers. I wanted the smooth slide of his cock all the way in and out. I wanted to fall apart in his arms.

He obliged. Lifting me as though I were nothing, taking care not to strain my bonds, he raised me so I could wrap my legs around his hips. The pronounced muscles there made me squeeze tighter so I could feel them. Holding me in place, he smacked against me, driving in. Then feathers, wings, stroked my back from both sides. The feathers felt enormous too. I pictured what Eros must look like now and nearly climaxed. The wings' caress played in my sweat-damp hair and down to my ass.

"Ye-es!" I cried before realizing I needed to.

"Fuck," he grunted. The wings closed around me like another set of arms.

Never, I'd never felt anything like this. My job was pleasure and I hadn't known the meaning.

"Psyche, fuck!" he cried again.

In the blind quiet of the room, our curses and the slap of our bodies made the only sounds. I bunched together around the point where we connected, squeezing his cock convulsively.

"Yes, come for me, Psyche," he panted.

He had noticed every flush and tremble of my body, called it out, lavished praise on every response.

My muscles trembled, bracing. Release built higher, like a scream that wouldn't crest into the open air. In the temple, I would have cried out already, but this impending eruption was real.

Eros increased his pace, his firm, flat stomach meeting mine with each thrust. His rod-hard cock hurt less as I welcomed him, wet and pleading.

With a final surge all the way in, he shattered me completely.

When I came to, Eros was still touching me, murmuring admiration for my body. His fingers, his breath, were all insatiable. His words made my skin tingle as much as his body did, hot against mine. "Ah yes, the taste of that pretty pink sex. You feel so good. So good." He seemed almost delirious.

But he had pulled out and I felt empty without him inside me. Soreness didn't deter me from flexing backward, my wrists and ankles still in their restraints, to present myself to him.

A dark chuckle accompanied the touch of wings at my back. He hiked me up so I could no longer feel his thick arousal against my bottom, and he cradled me against him.

Without sight, every other sense heightened—the sweaty heat of his muscular form, so much taller than I was, the musky sweet scent from his room and our sex, the sound of his breath softly blowing my hair. I should have incorporated blindfolds into my pleasure offerings at the temple.

"My gods," he breathed. His large hand covered most of the width of my back. "How else can I pleasure you?"

I was bound, imprisoned. We'd consummated our marriage. Yet he didn't leave. Or even let the restraints chafe any time he could help it.

Men of the temple got their pleasure and left satisfied. That was on a good day. Eros had his pleasure—it was obvious in that empty space inside me—but he stayed with me.

I drew in a deep, slow breath. The movement pressed us closer together, every point of contact humming, insisting I pay attention. The ridges of his hard muscles against my soft stomach. The place where our thighs touched. The tiny circles he drew on my back with his index finger.

Something like sadness entered with my breath. Why did I feel so good? I knew in advance that our sex would probably be pleasurable, but this moment wasn't sex. It was... what? He was just holding me, relishing the nearness of me.

And I felt safe.

That was ridiculous. My fingers had lost feeling from being suspended above my head. But as we breathed together, I couldn't deny it.

He felt safe.

I swallowed. Cytherea hadn't given me a knife yet, but my mission was still on. It was just that... I'd expected Eros to be more like the cruel men I'd known and killed before. But he wasn't.

You're just thinking that because of the mind-blowing sex, I reminded myself. It was easy to get caught up in pleasure. Pleasure brought a sense of nearness—one of the reasons Cytherea promoted it. But that didn't negate the fact that Eros was stealing worship from the queen, drying up her temples, and taking advantage of young women to choose as his bride.

When I spoke, I hardly recognized my own voice. It had grown croaky and deep. "My hand's fallen asleep. Can you take me down?"

Immediately, he reached up and took the hand I waved. His felt hot since mine was bloodless. A warm kiss followed, right on the palm. My senses were shaken for a moment. How tall was he? Taller than Zepherin? Well, his cock was huge, so why shouldn't all of him be bigger than I had realized?

"I can't release you yet," he said in a bitter undertone. Even that answer I didn't want to hear caressed me like velvet.

"Why not?" I whispered. "I like your bed."

A low sound emanated from his chest, more feeling than sound. I found a new point of contact between us as he grew harder again.

"Don't say things like that," he chastised, massaging my hand.

I had an opening, then. If I was ever going to fulfil Cytherea's command, I had to be unchained around him, not merely alone. "Don't say that I like your bed? Or that I want to feel your weight on top of me?"

"Stop." This time the command was gruff. He stepped away. Cold enveloped me. Didn't he want to be seduced by his wife? "In time," he said. "I have to go."

"Wait!"

Fabric rasped as he covered himself. Disappointment ate at me. I wanted more of him. My center felt sore because he'd claimed me so thoroughly and... I couldn't get enough. He'd found places nobody else had touched—nearly a miracle, considering the life I'd led.

Places that were now just for him.

"I can't," he replied. Then a sigh. He returned to run his hands over my sides, grazing the swell of my breasts with his thumbs. His kiss lingered, savoring rather than hungry. Those were the three places we touched: right hand, left hand, lips. It wasn't enough. The half-snarl he emitted when we broke the kiss showed he didn't think so either. So why was he leaving?

"When?" I croaked.

"Soon."

I didn't need to hear the door open and close to know that he had gone. The entire room felt vacant without him. Frigid.

My thoughts rampaged. To assassinate Eros for the goddess I needed my damn hand free. But the thought of freedom didn't bring violent fantasies to mind, but seductive ones. I had plenty of ideas for what to do with free hands and feet and sight. But I couldn't indulge those fantasies. Eros had wronged the queen. Eros-suna had sullied my city. His death meant my life.

But now that I had experienced the obsessive attention of the god of sex, could I ever give it up?

22

EROS

I couldn't form a thought. Not one thought. Only images and sensations. Her pussy, hot and slick, her helpless groans, her head thrown back, her body pounding against mine...

How had I said no to releasing Psyche from her bonds? *Why* had I said it?

Unreasoning annoyance gripped me in a fist, and I tried adjusting my wings in their restraints. When they wouldn't budge, I growled. Psyche made me feel free. Made the wait worth it. She'd only grown wilder when I'd held her with my wings as well as my hands. Most others didn't touch my wings when we made love. But she wanted that sensitive, rare part of me. I wanted her to grip the root of them, pulling along their length as far as she could reach while I topped her.

Gods, I could hardly catch my breath.

I needed assurances. The eclipse was coming and I needed to know that Lox would honor his promise to sponsor my bid for godhood. If I were a god, Cytherea wouldn't be able to kill me. Once she couldn't find new ways to end my life, I could live again, free Psyche, and banish the thick shadow of fear.

Mostly.

It wasn't only my life I feared for, but the betrayal of others that had become the norm. Even Psyche might run. But that was the risk of living. The smallest crumb of love opened the door to inevitable pain.

Familiar anxiety shot through the haze of my ebbing desire. I'd trusted Zepherin. I'd trusted Pothos. Hell, I'd even trusted Cytherea once.

I reached the room where the ceremony had taken place. A panel separated me from Irena as it had when she'd last visited. She sat gracefully in a chair, leafing through a stack of official documents. She raised her eyes when I entered.

"Considering your reputation, I expected you to be gone longer," she said, tone unreadable.

Sweat was still drying on my skin under the heavy cloak. "I have his nomination?" I asked, my voice low and hoarse.

"Two nominations."

I blinked. "What?"

Irena set down the pile of documents and stood. "Two nominations. For you and Psyche. You didn't think Lox would only nominate you, did you? That would defeat the purpose."

Because Psyche would die and I would still be a god who could make dangerous alliances.

How had this not been more obvious to me? Had I been so distracted with making my choice or with Zepherin's deception or with the prospect of satisfying my lust at last that I'd forgotten? Probably. Despite my caution, reasoning wasn't always my strong suit. That was the point of all my damned routines. I knew I couldn't trust myself to remember if I did things out of order.

"So you haven't told her she'll become a goddess?" Irena asked, quirking an amused brow.

"No." I felt stupid. And like I wanted to run back and never leave her arms. *A goddess...*

"It's both or nothing, Eros. If you bring her to Zenia, Lox will support you. If not, I'm afraid you're on your own."

I couldn't tell how she felt about that second option. Irena treated everyone fairly but sometimes fairness seemed callous.

"I want her to be a goddess." And I meant it. God-marriages were eternal, which normally would have made me shy away, but Psyche, more than anyone else I'd ever met, was a partner I would gamble my fate on. Maybe it was the chaos talking. I didn't care.

"Very well. I'll see you at the eclipse."

A smile tugged at my lips, soured by the recent pangs of guilt and anger it took to get here. I missed Zepherin. If he had simply asked to be with Cressida, would I have allowed it after I calmed down? Now that I'd chosen Psyche, I felt sure I would. But he hadn't given me that chance.

It all mattered less now that Psyche was mine. She *wanted* to be mine. No coercion or sadness. She offered her body to me with abandon, and I couldn't wait to taste her again and tell her the good news.

23

PSYCHE

Eros called for me again a few hours later. This time there was little preamble. The scent of him made me molten before the first touch. This time, he ordered me bound to the bed. It was so, so much better than the last time I'd lain there. The heavy insistence of him, the way he knew how to move and responded to my every shiver and cry... He was memorizing me. No one had tried to understand my exact mechanisms before.

Kissing the crook of my elbow aroused me more than kissing my neck. There was a particular tempo—not fast or slow, but firm and grinding—that I needed most. Asking me what I wanted and praising me for my flexibility, my taste, and my reactions made me pulsate wider. It took him no time to figure out those pieces of my desire and reduce me to a whimpering, writhing mess on the blankets.

In his hands, sex was an art. I recognized another artist, one better than I was, though I could demonstrate him some things if I were free. I wanted to show off. And apparently, I had time.

Still no knife.

And a naughty part of me was very glad.

Afterward, he lay beside me, panting, one hand still gently exploring the front of my body. "I have something to tell you," he said between breaths.

My heartbeat, already fast, throbbed harder. "What?" Would he finally free my hands? Take off the blindfold? Admit his identity?

"I've been... hiding away for a long time. But I've found a way to stop running."

I held my breath as I strained to listen to his low, husky words, warm against my ear.

"You are my wife now, love, but you're human. I've secured a way for both of us to become gods. Then I won't have to run anymore." He smoothed sweaty strands of hair from my forehead. "We'll be safe, and I can release you. You can even..." To my surprise, emotion clogged his words and he faltered.

"Can even what?" I whispered.

"See my face."

I could hardly take in what he was telling me. Become gods? I could be one of the deathless? The idea was laughable. And it would never come true. A short life of freedom and peace meant more than an immortal life bound to Cytherea's enemy.

Didn't it?

"I want to see your face," I said truthfully, for all the competing reasons within me.

If one could hear a smile, then I did. Eros planted a kiss,

soft and full, on my cheek. "At the eclipse, we'll go to Zenia. It's only a few days away."

Something clicked into place. The timing was too perfect. Did our marriage have something to do with his ability to ascend to godhood? Was that why he made his decision so quickly after demanding candidates for his bride?

The part of my soul that had softened toward him hardened once again. If Eros became a god, I wouldn't be able to complete Cytherea's task. Ever. And I'd be married to him for eternity.

"How many days?" I asked, summoning all the smoothness I'd learned in the temple to keep my voice from trembling.

"Two. We'd have to leave tomorrow and the ceremony is the day after that."

Two days. I couldn't kill Eros on Zenia. I'd be stranded. I wouldn't know how to return for Cytherea's promised reward.

Eros' light touch traced up to the place above my heart. My pulse thrashed against his palm. "What are you feeling?" he asked gently.

"I don't deserve to be a goddess." My answer surprised me, but as soon as it was out, I knew it was true. The best I could hope for after my many sins and inadequacies was the queen's protection. That, I could accept.

Eros hummed against the crook of my neck. "Then maybe you're right for it. You're my goddess." Teeth closed lightly on my earlobe.

My belly flipped as he nipped at me, taking his time. "You don't know me," I replied. Gods, I needed to stop saying whatever was in my head. The next thing out of my mouth would be damning. But I'd never been careful enough. Or even just... enough.

"But you'll always be my demi-god," I added.

If my hand had been free, I would have run it down my face in shame at how stupid that sounded coming out of my mouth.

The teeth stopped. Whether he was angry or amused or suspicious, I couldn't tell. "You're right," he finally said, "but I want to know you. We'll have lifetimes. You'll be safe with me."

My throat worked. Safe. Safe with Eros was a lie. A delicious, delicious lie.

"Want me to show you?" He was on top of me again, already hard for another round.

"Yes."

I could put off worrying for another moment while he learned more facets of what made me grip what I could reach of the blankets in trembling fists.

HALF-DAZED, I RETURNED TO MY ROOM. AS SOON AS I SHUT the door against Olitor, who continued to be my new guardian, I leaned my forehead on the cool wood. *I've secured a way for both of us to become gods.* My mind spun. *Could* I be safe with Eros, as he claimed?

"Psyche."

I jolted and whirled. A familiar young man with golden

skin stood at the foot of my bed. In his hands lay a red cushion. On the cushion, with a glittering handle of silver and pearls, was a long knife.

My muscles braced at the sight of it. This was the mission I'd prepared for. So why did I feel sick?

"Is it him?" the youth asked.

"Yes."

"Have you seen him?"

"No, but I know it's him."

"Then good luck."

24

PSYCHE

I stood alone in my room, clutching the knife. The hilt felt too hard and solid against my palm. Like the rock behind the temple after those men had grabbed me. I'd needed something solid then. But now...

I had no time to think. Eros was leaving for Zenia in only two days. Once he did that, my future would be gone with no chance of retrieval. Still, I wanted more time—more time to learn about Eros, if he really was the monster everyone feared. Eros-suna hadn't made life in Card easy for women. How much of that was Eros' fault?

He did nothing to stop it from happening. With that reminder, I tightened my grip on the knife. My mind was cloudy from a staggeringly good fuck. That was all.

I would obey my goddess. It wasn't as if I hadn't killed before. The memory brought on a wash of shame, even though the men I'd slaughtered deserved to die.

No, I definitely didn't deserve to be a goddess.

As the minutes wore away, the plan building since I'd

arrived took shape. I would wait until the deepest part of night, sneak back to Eros' chamber, and stab him as he slept.

The night passed in feverish anticipation. Without windows, I had to guess the time. My nerves sang so loudly that five minutes felt as long as an hour. Time stretched and morphed in odd ways as I stood wavering near the door, the dagger in my sweaty fist. The idea of stowing it in my clothes to hide it in case I came upon someone in the hallway felt even more reckless than holding it the whole way. What if I couldn't draw it out again? In my confusion, it seemed like the blade would be lost if it left my sight for even a moment. I'd hold it. If someone saw me, I'd get in trouble with or without the knife.

It had to be late now. The air felt stifling, still. Or maybe I was just holding my breath.

With utter recklessness, I swung open the door, brandishing the knife. *Straight down the hall, then one turn.* I exited the common area and entered the antiseptic hallway. Cool gray stone and metal formed the space. No plants grew like there were in the common area. It felt more natural to close my eyes and feel my way forward, since I'd taken that path so often without seeing anything, but I if I did that, I couldn't be sure of going straight.

Whenever I started to doubt myself with the sight of a new place, I paused to smell and listen.

An arch opened to my right. That was the way. My hand grew numb as I traced the path back to Eros' room. I didn't think about him. I couldn't.

Then, the door. His door. I was outside my body, acting on necessity, like a puppet being maneuvered by a greater hand.

Cytherea's, I supposed. After this, everything would be all right.

I pressed my ear to the door. No sound came from inside. Not a surprise, since no sound came from the entire empty fortress.

My fingers twisted the handle. It gave with a tiny click. I froze. My head pounded with the need to hear. But there was still nothing.

Did he even sleep in here? I assumed, because of the bed, but maybe he had beds in several rooms. Lust was his domain, after all.

With one eye, I peeked into the darkness within. An upward facing window let in blue moonlight. It was so much lighter than the hallway that I cringed, but no one moved to acknowledge me. A bow and arrows hung on the wall beside a massive brown cloak. My gaze trailed down to the bed, where a huge, magnificent shape lay.

When Eros didn't stir, I gathered enough bravery to enter. During sex, he always knew when my pulse spiked or breath caught. Could he hear my hammering heart now?

As I approached, moonlight silvered the figure so I could see him clearly. Eros lay on his stomach, arms flung out carelessly, along with a pair of enormous white wings that anchored into a pale, muscled back. He was completely naked. A firm, shapely buttocks tapered down to strong legs and clean feet. He slept with one knee at an angle like a climber. And his face. It was turned so I could see it, crowned with long golden hair. He had a straight nose and full, sensual lips. The way the light hit the bow of them did something to me. His eyes were closed, rimmed with long, almost feminine lashes.

His entire body spoke of excess. Those wide hands were made to touch, those lips to kiss.

And they had kissed *me*. I'd experienced that body, but even I hadn't pictured it this perfect.

More than that, I'd vowed myself to this being, so much more magnificent than I was.

I mentally shook myself. Still standing by the door, I swallowed and rotated the dagger in my hand. This was the trap of the Eros-suna. There was more to life than beauty. Peace, for example, mattered more. But as I considered the act I was about to attempt, it felt impossible. His back corded so thick with muscle that I might not have the strength to plunge the knife all the way through to his heart. It was too risky. I'd have to cut his neck. A surge of nausea threatened to make me vomit. With effort, I suppressed my sickness and treaded carefully forward, avoiding the gorgeous wings that took up a healthy portion of the room.

One strike. I'd slice once, as hard as I could, and it would be done.

My eyes stung as I drew close. His soothing words echoed in my head like a nightmare I wanted to curl up into.

This was a crush, that was all. Natural, given what we'd done together. Once I was free, none of it would matter.

My stomach felt like a ball of ice as I watched a vein lightly pulsing in his strong neck. The jaw above it could cut as surely as the knife I held.

What did his eyes look like? The question struck me as important, even while I knew it was just a meaningless plea to stay this execution. It didn't matter what his eyes looked like.

They were dark and bright at once, piercing.

Panicked.

I stumbled backward but Eros was faster. My back hit the wall behind me, and an arrowhead dug into the flesh just above my collarbone. My weapon clattered to the floor. Eros held me in place, his expression a mask of grief and rage. The weapon in his hand trembled. I felt it break the skin.

"What were you doing?" he growled in a voice that said he already knew but hated the answer. His eyes were red and wild now.

My blood raced frantically. He pressed himself harder against me, feathers fanning up and out until all I could see was Eros' golden head, painfully beautiful, against a wall of white.

I couldn't answer. He would kill me if I said it out loud.

The door wasn't far. I had to run. Maybe then I could get the dagger again somehow and...

I stopped thinking. Now was the time to *move*. With a desperate cry, I shoved his chest with all my might. Despite throwing my entire weight against him, I barely succeeded in moving him at all. His bare flesh felt warm and firm under my hands.

This was the first time I'd touched him. And the first time we'd looked each other in the face.

He seemed to realize it too, because something shifted in his expression, unsure in a new way. He drove the point of the arrow a little deeper into the skin above my collarbone, but not enough to actually wound. He kept eye contact as he did it. If I didn't know better, I'd think he was... hungry.

I was angry and afraid, but hunger hit me too like a strong

wave, pulling me down as I fought against it. I struggled against my captor but he was so much bigger than I was, so strong, that I couldn't escape unless he allowed it. He was naked and beautiful and he had ruined my chance at happiness.

His arrow wasn't really hurting me, although I felt a trickle of blood oozing down to my neckline. If he wanted to kill me, he could have done it already. The places where we touched burned. Emboldened, I growled in his face, daring him to do something. I had nothing left to lose.

His gaze blazed with red rage, with desire, with everything. He was a never-satisfied flame.

His body tensed, twitched, then he cast away the arrow, exchanging it for my short hair. He forced me to tilt my chin up to meet his gaze, but even this grip was firm, frustrated, but not harsh.

Lust glazed my senses as I looked at him and found an urgent, angry wanting there. I pushed him away once more, then gripped his sides and pressed him hard against me. His face followed, meeting mine in a savage kiss. I half-expected biting, punishment, but instead we kissed like we were lovers who would never get the chance to touch each other again. Which we were.

I couldn't get close enough. I reached over his powerful shoulder to touch the wings, to pull those closer too.

Eros roared and scooped me up by the back of the knees, practically throwing me on the bed. I finally got to see his front as he stalked forward like an avenging angel, all defined muscle and smooth gold-tinged skin and—yes, there it was. Just as big as it had felt.

He was passion and beauty and lust, and I feared him, and I hated him, and *oh gods* how I wanted him.

Before he could crawl toward me, I got up on my knees to meet him, grabbing for him to get closer, reaching for his hard length. My fist didn't quite reach around it. By the time I started pumping and touching all of him I could reach with my other hand, his cock was already wet. His answering moan made my core vibrate. He didn't have words now. Neither of us could say anything or we'd break the spell. I was assassin and he was target. But I needed him to make that sound again, to spread his wings wide with pleasure—no, they were contracting inward now. We were in a dream with nothing but sensation. I pulled and sucked pleasure from him as if it would give me life. His cries were loud and angry and I didn't care if anyone heard us. I'd fallen past the edge of consequences. All I had was this moment, that patch of skin, this kiss, that sound of ripping as my clothes came off.

I held his back, felt his muscles slide under the skin as he moved into me. My fingers threaded through the feathers.

"Higher," he grated.

I felt upward, finally gripping the place where his wings met his back as though I would haul myself up underhand.

Instantly, I felt his reaction. His abs stiffened and a choked sound burst from his wicked mouth.

I pulled down harder. His broken cry grew thin and high. Experimenting, I stroked farther out. He was trembling now. Then, finally, I returned to the base, where the muscles protruded to anchor the weight of the wings, and pressed upward.

A cry of surprise and he arched backward. When I pushed

harder, his breath froze, gorgeous face contorting into a mask of piercing pleasure.

I released him, pulling him to me. I needed his body on mine, his lips on mine again. This time, his movements were more worshipful than angry, but desperation—the last-chance feeling—surrounded us like fog.

We clung to each other, adjusting and readjusting our hands. I was amazed he'd lasted this long after his eyes had rolled back and his mouth had opened in that silent scream when I fondled his wings.

Maybe he didn't want to think either.

No thoughts. Just this.

When we did start to break, it was in inarticulate cries. Protests. Adoration. Exclamations with more conversation in them than words. We didn't want to stop. I wanted to struggle together like this forever.

I broke first. More than once.

Then, with a growl more animal than man, he did too.

And we were left alone with the truth.

25

EROS

Psyche looked at me hard and held me with all her free limbs as the air chilled around us. Her expression turned fearfully defiant, a milder dare than she'd given me when I held the arrow against her skin.

Psyche, my Psyche, had tried to kill me. How we ended up here, I hardly knew. I just knew my heart was blackening, growing heavier the longer we stayed in silence.

My first reaction had been instinct. I'd countered attacks like this before. But then the hand that held the knife was Psyche's, and I couldn't kill her to defend myself. My body simply wouldn't do it. It felt wrong, even worse than when Pothos had betrayed me.

While we clung together, grappling and desperate, I kept expecting a blade to appear in Psyche's hand. I almost would have welcomed it this time.

Her dark eyes still fixed on me. They were incredible eyes, deep enough for me to lose myself. Was she waiting for me to pronounce judgment on her? To let her go?

I considered easing up on my knees to give her more space, but she held me down with a fierceness I didn't understand. Her small hands splayed just underneath the joint of my wings.

Since when did *I* have to say something? She snuck up on me. She... I couldn't dwell on the pain of the betrayal or else horror would own me. But now I could think of nothing else.

"Did..." I cleared my throat. It felt as raw as if I'd screamed for hours. "Did she force you to do this?"

She didn't answer for a long moment. "Who?"

"Cytherea." I couldn't help but spit her name.

"The goddess?" Anger flashed in her lovely eyes. So much life in them, so much intelligence and desire and...

I needed to stop thinking like this. "It was her, wasn't it?"

"It was... my choice." Her grip loosened enough for me to angle upright. Without her heated skin against mine, I felt freezing. She shivered too. But that could have been fear. She just admitted to trying to kill a demi-god.

Even though I knew that, after so long without any physical contact at all, I needed to touch her like I needed air.

That was when I noticed it. The mark between her breasts that looked as though a piercing belonged there. A piercing. Something to mar her perfect skin in deference to the goddess.

Psyche was a temple courtesan.

I hadn't known there were lower depths for me to fall into.

Revelations washed in relentlessly.

I couldn't let Psyche out of my sight, but I was leaving for Zenia to become a god in hours. Lox wouldn't support my nomination unless she became a goddess too. Then our marriage would last forever, not just the length of her mortal life.

If I'd been strangled with ropes, it wouldn't have felt worse. Cytherea had finally caught me. I had nowhere to go unless I submitted to execution.

"Psyche." Her name was a quiet plea on my tongue. She was the only one who could comfort me. I wanted her to hold me. But she... she didn't want me after all. She was a professional, practicing her pleasure-offerings to Cytherea. My entire being felt suspended.

Then a choked laugh escaped my mouth. "I thought maybe Gia would do this. Not you."

"I've known this whole time." Her eyes flashed fire, but her voice was soft.

My mind didn't work. It barely grasped my own predicament, could much less decide what to do about it.

Finally, from the depths of my being came a protest, a scream. Enough. I'd had *enough*. This was the lowest Cytherea had stooped to punish me for something I couldn't control.

Rulers of all Eight Realms congregated in Zenia every decade for the eclipse. Cytherea would be there too. One way or another, I would end this. Either I would get safety and freedom, or I'd die trying. No more of this half-life.

"This was always for her," I snarled. Even now, it was hard to believe it, looking down at Psyche's face. It wasn't hatred burning her cheeks red. But she tipped her head in a barely visible nod.

I ran my fingers through her dark hair, sweeping it away from her forehead firmly enough to massage her scalp. My chaos within reached a peak. I'd break this time.

Suddenly resolved, I grabbed her upper arm and did something I hadn't for a long time. I traveled through the air like the demi-god I was. The sensation touched me like fingers.

We landed, naked, in a different part of the fortress. Olitor's room. Psyche, still held down by me straddling her hips, widened her eyes as she took in the new space.

"Olitor!" I cried, hauling Psyche to her feet. She was so much smaller in reality than she loomed in my thoughts. I bit back an apology for launching her up so quickly.

A gasp and bucking shadow. "My lord!" came the raspy response from the bed.

"Bind her," I commanded, "and don't let her go back to her room. Don't worry about the blindfold. Keep her restrained here until I'm ready to retrieve her."

Then we'd go to Zenia together. To confront Cytherea directly for the first time in fifty years. And, maybe, to become gods.

26

PSYCHE

I couldn't stop shaking. Olitor had obeyed Eros' order to bind me, not even offering me any clothing. The gardener acted a little too enthusiastic about the assignment. My wrists were secured behind my back, and my ankles were tied together with only enough room to shuffle forward if I needed to. A rope connected the length between my feet to a collar around my neck. A final cord anchored to the collar would probably serve as a kind of leash. For now, it fastened me to a torch ring in the wall.

I sat in the shadowy corner, trying to make sense of things. Eros hadn't killed me for attempting to stab him, but he had imprisoned me.

I deserved it. For everything I'd done and for everything I'd almost done. I didn't want Eros to die. Not anymore.

What was he going to do with me? I'd seen his face. I knew his identity and I'd tried to kill him on behalf of the goddess. Gory evidence on the mountain showed what he was willing to do to protect himself. So, why had he kept me alive? It couldn't be because of the angry, desperate sex we had. That had felt more like a goodbye than anything.

As hours passed without Eros, I felt grateful that Olitor didn't touch me after tying me up. He returned frequently, though, to make sure I hadn't escaped.

Was Eros simply deciding what to do with me, or would he bring me with him to Zenia for the eclipse, as he originally planned?

"We'll have lifetimes. You'll be safe with me."

Heat pricked at the corners of my eyes. I'd never be safe. No matter what I tried, how good I strove to be, how much I sacrificed, I was always cast out alone.

For the first time in years, I cried. Heavy sobs racked my body. Tears streamed in torrents down my face and I couldn't even wipe them away. The attacks, the lies, the dismissals, and now this—getting so close to goddess-blessed peace, only to have it ripped away one final time.

And Eros. He was pleasure incarnate, but he was more than that. We both exaggerated our feelings for each other, I was sure, but there was a kernel of bald truth in what we said and what we did for each other. I... loved him. Despite the man's corpse on the mountain and his demand for brides and even my situation now. Maybe it was absurd, but he struck me as someone who merely craved love and safety.

Just like me.

I had no hope of a happy ending, so, once my tears slowed, I allowed my mind to wander wherever it wanted. Nothing mattered anymore. If I wanted to fantasize about a different outcome, why should I censor myself? The fantasy that staved away the darkness best was one where Eros forgave me, understood me, and we were able to rebuild something together, free from pain. In that story, I was like Cytherea, sensual and strong, forging my own future.

Hopefully the goddess would forgive me for failing. I'd tried my best. But my best was never enough.

I STOOD IN THE TEMPLE, MY VERTICAL PIERCING BACK IN place. Above me, the great statue of Cytherea loomed.

When the goddess looked down at me, I realized I wasn't alone. The other courtesans, all topless, congregated in the shadowy recesses near the water basin. There were Phoebe and Castor. They didn't seem to notice Cytherea had moved. What were they staring at? Me?

Did they... know?

I looked down at my hands. Blood and brain matter gloved them as they had that day behind the temple. Bile rose up in my throat. Frantically, I tried to scrub them off on my skirt, but it was light-colored and thin. All I managed to do was stain that too. My breathing came out ragged as I rubbed the blood off on my torso instead. Cytherea, with her empty stone eyes, watched my struggle.

There was never less blood, only more. My whole body was smeared and my hands were no cleaner. Why? Why wouldn't it come off?

Tears bit my eyes. In the haze, something gold caught my attention.

As one, the attention of all the watchers shifted to the ground to the right of my bloodstained feet.

It was Eros, his beautiful white wings broken under him. His body almost looked small compared to them, curled on its side, eyes tight shut, golden hair unfurling from his bloodied head.

"No!" I knelt by one wing that had broken at the top joint. The feathers felt soft but cold under my fingertips.

The statue of Cytherea bent closer.

And a slow smile transformed her stone face.

I gasped and shuddered awake. The real Eros stood near Olitor's door, peering down at me, his hair swept up in a topknot. He wore an old-style outfit that draped over one shoulder and flowed to his feet, probably to make room for his wide, unbroken wings. On his bare bicep he wore a golden cuff. The light color of the fabric and the golden accents only served to highlight his allure and the depth of his eyes. He was all sensual lines and firm muscles.

Still recovering from the dream, I tucked my knees more tightly to my chest. My face felt puffy from crying. If he still wanted to go to Zenia, he'd have to do it without my being fit to see any gods.

As if he could read my thoughts, he set a brown satchel on the floor. "Get changed."

"You"—I sniffed—"you didn't send Olitor." *You came your-self.* What did that mean?

His throat tightened visibly and he lifted his chin. The new angle made him look ten times taller and more imperious, but there was a softness around the edges of his eyes. It had been there even when he held me against the wall with an arrow to my throat. Reluctance, or something else.

"We're going to Zenia," he said.

"Will—?"

"I don't know. Just get dressed."

I blinked away the tears shimmering at the edges of my vision and flexed my toes. He had ordered me tied up. I couldn't change unless he released me.

Clenching his jaw, he approached and crouched in front of me. With a natural physicality that made it hard to look away, he untied my ankles first, his knuckles making only the barest contact against my skin. The muscles in his arms shifted as he moved to my collar. My heartbeat juddered in my neck. He probably noticed. He never seemed to miss any detail of me. When he straightened, so did I. Obediently, I turned around so he could release the cord binding my wrists.

With eye contact broken, he allowed himself to touch my upturned palms and trace a line at my wrist.

Neither of us spoke as he reestablished distance between us. My eyes fell once again on the brown bag. He kicked it closer, not moving to leave. Inside was a silky dress much like those I had worn in this fortress already. The only difference was that this one shone a bright, pure gold. I furrowed my brow. Was he claiming me by covering me a matching color?

I released a breath of a laugh. We were married. We had claimed each other, not only in our vows, but in every way. Except love and trust.

The dress slipped on and I rubbed grittiness out of my eyes, as ready as I could be.

"Turn," he said softly.

I rotated all the way around.

His chest heaved with a heavy breath, pain heavy in the sound. And he offered me his arm.

I stared at it, then up at him. Did he really think I'd take it? With time to cool down, he might have realized that he should kill me for almost killing him.

Maybe in Zenia, he would become a god and crush me decisively. After everything that happened, there was no way he wanted to make me a goddess.

When why bring me the dress at all? I wasn't thinking straight.

I reached out and placed my hand on his forearm. As soon as I touched his warm skin, I felt him tense hard beneath my fingers.

And, with a rush of suffocating darkness, we disappeared.

27

EROS

My chest squeezed as we crossed the expanse of the Corae Sea. I'd only crossed it a few times and never like this—with a lovely, murderous wife on my arm.

I held in a grunt as we finally landed in a large, circular, honey-scented room with a stone floor lined with huge antique vases stamped with lightning symbols. I tucked in my wings to avoid knocking into them. The distance was even longer than I remembered. Maybe it was my nerves. Maybe it was Psyche. Maybe it was that I knew fuck-all about what I was going to do now that I was here.

I'd never attended an eclipse in Zenia. I'd heard about the ceremony, of course. Once in a decade, gods and goddesses of the Realms met to inaugurate new gods if any humans or demigods passed scrutiny. I only knew pieces of what the ceremony entailed—the eclipse, probably, because of the timing, some kind of sacrifice...

I never expected to become a god. Before Cytherea's

attacks, I hadn't wanted to. Life as a demi-god on the western coast suited me.

But now the options were to ascend and escape her wrath, or die by one of her attacks.

Psyche let go of my arm, leaving burning trails where her fingers had gripped me. Her tan skin flushed from the trip. I felt her heartbeat quicken and temperature rise just short of panic.

Maybe I could find Lox himself before the ceremony and explain what had happened. Irena had said he wouldn't sponsor my nomination without a mortal queen ascending too. But surely...

My thoughts fizzed away. The chance of Lox changing his mind was slim at best. In the next few hours, I had to decide whether both of us or neither of us became gods.

My mood darkened. Already this trip was a disaster. I never should have come in the first place.

At least my endless hiding would stop now, one way or another.

"This is Zenia?"

Psyche's question brought me back to myself.

"Yes. This is King Thenios' palace."

Amazement filled her wide brown eyes as they skimmed over the massive vases. This was the arrival chamber. We had to get out in case more guests appeared.

"The ceremony is tomorrow," I explained. "All the gods will be here." *All the gods.* As if a light had struck, I knew what to do. "Come with me."

My torment had started with Cytherea. It would end with

her too. I suspected she'd be here early, even if she didn't show her face until some dramatic moment.

"Where are—?"

"To Cytherea, your goddess." I couldn't keep the sneer out of my voice.

Psyche's mouth dropped open and her heart hammered faster than before. She actually trembled. Immediately, I regretted my words. I fisted my hands to keep from reaching out to comfort her. But her trembling wasn't only due to fear. There was hope there too.

So many emotions roiled through me when I looked at her that I didn't know what to do with myself.

Whenever I looked at Psyche, I didn't see a murderer. I saw my magnetic chosen bride, brave and intriguing. Though she didn't look at me, her bright, curious eyes drew mine as she kept pace. I shivered at the memory of when they were covered. She hadn't faked her passion for me when I had to hold her up to get all the way inside her. She hadn't dived for discarded weapons after I caught her hovering over me with a knife.

I was being stupid. But Psyche's presence wrapped around me like warm covers. Even now, peering at her from the corner of my eye, I wanted more of her. Just the two of us. If only I could go back in time and erase what Psyche had done, or do something to pluck out her loyalty to my enemy. Pain pressed on my chest and I rubbed at it like a sore muscle.

At the threshold of the arrival chamber, I froze. If I stepped out, I'd be completely exposed. I hadn't brought my wing straps, cloak, or gloves. They lay haphazardly strewn around my bedroom in Aphriso. A large swath of bare skin stretched from my arm up to my chest. Nothing protected my wings. I sucked in a slow breath.

I realized I was stalling when Psyche caught my eye. A precious line formed between her brows. Could that really be concern written there? What assassin cared about their victim?

I exhaled carefully.

And stepped out.

The air smelled like honey out here too, in this bright corridor. I let it flow over my skin. Suddenly, all I wanted to do was stretch my wings as far as they would go to brush the opposite walls. I almost laughed at the image of other death-less beings dodging out of the way. I indulged myself with one aching stretch and a flutter before marching forward, Psyche taking two steps for every one of mine.

I still had to focus on breathing—the air seemed thick now that unvetted strangers were in it—but it got easier with every step. There were dark-skinned mer-people from Nalia, bronze warriors from Eriset, diplomats from Kantharos, and others I couldn't place, who had wings or fur or antlers. One woman might have been a vampire. Many strange beings, but none terrifying. I missed being in the company of so many. I'd had only a few servants at arm's length and my own chaotic mind for years.

No one attacked. I received a few appreciative looks. Psyche did too.

She watched other demi-gods pass, breathless. I loved that expression of awe on her face. I'd seen it before, but more acute, right after I'd slammed her against the wall. Wonder bordering on reverence. She had drunk me in like a thirsty dog laps water. The feeling was mutual.

Stop. Getting caught in Psyche's orbit every time my brain functioned wasn't doing me any favors. One person was responsible for ruining our chance at bliss, and I was going to confront her.

Do things in order. With effort, I tamed my thoughts, imagined they were a cloth covered in a pattern of hares. *Find Cytherea first.*

Cytherea wasn't in this grand hallway with its soaring pillars. In fact, I hadn't seen any of the eight rulers yet, but I knew where Cytherea would be. The God-King's palace had gigantic towers for each ruler. Hers probably had fucking swans in it.

Find her. Don't get distracted. I held out my hand to Psyche. She took it automatically, and I stepped through the air.

The movement caught Psyche off guard this time. Even though it was a shorter distance, she stumbled when we landed in Cytherea's tower. I squeezed Psyche's hand to keep her upright.

"I'm here!" I shouted into the lofted white hall, releasing Psyche's hand. I felt as if I were in a whale skeleton. Ribs reached to a peaked ceiling. Pillows didn't make the frosty furniture any more inviting. I stalked forward to the next room. Blood red flowers stood in a vase. It might as well have been the blood of Zepherin's company of soldiers as they protected my palace. Or the thin drop that slid from Psyche's perfect throat as instinct forced me against her with that arrow.

I pursed my lips in disgust. "Cytherea! You wanted me. Here I am!"

A stirring of fabric.

Cytherea appeared, in a dress that couldn't be called pink. Pink was a soft color and this was not a soft dress. The structured bodice tapered to points to cover her breasts and the skirt had a train as long as Cytherea was tall. A pearlescent crown towered on her blonde head.

Psyche fell on her face before the goddess, who gazed impassively down.

My blood seethed. Cytherea had tried to execute me for years and now she wouldn't even meet my eyes. Was she even surprised to see me confronting her in her own chambers?

"Here, look!" I cried, pointing at Psyche. My stomach clenched to see her like that, small on the ground. I'd thought... But I was wrong. "You got what you wanted. Here she is. I chose your temple girl for my wife and now she wants me dead. I'm done with this! I'm done hiding." I hated the taste of the words and the way my voice broke with anger and heartbreak when I said them.

Cytherea regarded Psyche coolly. "My temple girl? I've never seen this person."

Psyche's head jerked up just as the goddess turned away from her.

"You sent her to kill me," I said, throat dry. Did Cytherea really not know her? That was impossible. My gaze ricocheted from one to the other, trying to suss out the truth.

"My son, your paranoia has turned you delusional."

I bristled, shaking out my wings. "I'm not delusional. Do

you think I've lived in hiding for fifty years because I'm deluded about how much you want me dead?"

"Of course I want you dead," she replied, the picture of calm. "And yet you barge into my suite with nothing more than some... temple girl, you said?"

I was shaking. I felt my heartbeat in my adam's apple. "Not some temple girl," I said, regretting my earlier words. "My wife. You poisoned my wife."

"She appears well to me." The gaze she fixed on me dripped with venom, forcibly reminding me I wasn't a full god yet.

Footsteps shuffled behind us. Guards. It had to be. Cytherea looked past me, but I refused to take my eyes off her.

"Stay out of my way, Eros," she said. "I don't know why you're here, but if it's for the reason I think, you should crawl back to the hole you came from. No one would support a god of lust, a god of *chaos* who could never die."

I almost said Lox's name, but I bit it back. Better to make it a surprise. I peeled back my lips in a smile. "Tomorrow, that's exactly what you'll have."

I could become a god, but that didn't mean I felt safe. I was a bird in sight of hunters. I should have brought my bow. Cytherea didn't motion to her guards. They were a small matter compared to the women in the room with me. There stood my cruel mother, who had ruined my life by ripping away everyone I thought I could trust, and beside me Psyche rocked up on her knees with red eyes. Her straight black hair waved around her chin, framing the devastation on her face. My heart and body were utterly exposed.

I lowered my voice until it was little more than a growl. "You put her up to this. You can deny it, but I know it's true. She wouldn't have agreed to marry me if you hadn't suggested it." The truth of that statement pierced like a blade.

I'd gone past the point of recklessness. Maybe I would die here. If these were my last moments, I knew who I wanted to spend them with.

Setting my jaw, I offered to help Psyche to her feet. Would she defy her goddess by accepting my help?

Psyche's gaze flitted between the two of us. Maybe it was unfair of me to make her choose in this moment. Goddess, demi-god, human. Psyche didn't have the power here. But, to me, she did. Her choice meant everything.

"I chose her, knowing she had a little chaos," I said quietly, looking at my bride. Strangely, I trusted her. This was how I got in trouble with my lovers. But even though Psyche had tried to kill me, even though she'd hidden her connection to Cytherea, I believed her now as she tipped her distraught face up to meet mine with a look of determination. "And I choose her now."

She placed her delicate fingers in my hand. My pulse responded, rushing warmth through my entire body. Psyche rose, and I wove our fingers together as we faced Cytherea. A low flame of hope burned in my core. Did this mean Psyche loved me? At least it meant we stood united against Cytherea's tyranny. For now, that was more than enough.

Cytherea's perfect mouth curled in a mocking smile. "I'm glad for you. Now you can fear every night that your wife will kill you of her own accord."

But I was done with fear. Better death than a life of cowering, a life without intimacy and love. I was made for intimacy. If that meant danger, so be it.

"Not after we're god and goddess."

❧ 28 ❧

PSYCHE

I felt as deflated as an empty bag. Cytherea denied knowing anything about me. And I'd done all of this *for her*. I'd given myself up to the monster of the mountain and seduced Eros all to please her. And then I married him just to get him alone so I could kill him.

For her.

And she would still abandon me? Someone who worshipped her for as long as I could remember? This was crueller than any other abandonment I'd suffered. My extended family, the temple courtesans... They were human, but Cytherea had always given me hope. She made me feel strong and powerful, sexy. She gave my life meaning.

When I looked up from my deep bow, I saw no compassion in her eyes. I knew the gods could be vicious, but not like this.

I became aware of Eros' big fingers woven through mine, and I held them tighter. All this time, I had thought Cytherea was my key to freedom, but maybe, despite the Eros-suna making life worse in Card, Eros was the better being. I'd tried to stab him and he hadn't exacted vengeance. Instead, he'd given me another chance. He chose not to abandon me.

He loved me.

Cytherea's perfect mouth curled in a mocking smile. What would Phoebe and the other courtesans think if they could see me now? "I'm glad for you," she sneered at him. Her own son. How had I not known about their connection before? And how could anyone be so cruel to their own blood? "Now you can fear every night that your wife will kill you of her own accord."

I would kill to protect myself, but in this moment, Eros was protecting me. All the bondage and the searches and the blindfolds had been because he feared this goddess. Not because he was cruel. He had every right to order me dead or at least banish me, but he stood beside me, magnificent, and held my hand as we faced Cytherea together.

"Not after we're god and goddess," he replied.

Breath caught in my throat. Eros still wanted to go through with his plan? Was he bluffing?

But Eros was a terrible liar. Even fearing for his life, the best he could do was cover himself up. Whenever he spoke about his "hideous form", it sounded laughable.

He sounded believable now.

God and goddess.

Cytherea was terrifying and wrong and my heart broke because of it, but she'd still inspired me to be strong and feminine and unafraid. Even if I'd invented all those qualities in my own mind, I could try to live up to them now. I pictured the temple statue with its massive shield.

If it was true—if Eros and I really became gods at this ceremony—I could choose to embody what I'd always looked up to.

Cytherea's ocean eyes grew stormy. "If no one will nominate a god of lust, then imagine what they'll think of her."

I drew myself up and forced myself to meet her gaze. Swallowing, I forced out, in as clear a voice as I could muster, "Goddess of spirit."

A dimple appeared in Eros' cheek. The ground where we stood seemed to get steadier.

"We'll see you tomorrow at the ceremony," he said, and we flashed away from the white tower.

We hit the ground of the arrival chamber again, both breathless. My mind spun wildly but the first thing out of my mouth was "I'm sorry." I reached for his other hand. It was strong and soft, enveloping mine. I looked into his devastating eyes. "I'm sorry for everything. I didn't know."

He drew me forward, holding me against his chest. "You didn't know," he soothed, stroking my hair. Gentle lips touched the top of my head. "My goddess of spirit." A smile curled around the words.

"Do you think—?"

"It's perfect."

Cytherea wrenched my world apart when she dismissed me, but one thing hadn't broken. This. Us. By rights we should be at each other's throats. I still had questions and doubts, but Eros' arms still felt like the safest place to be.

"And," I ventured, "the Eros-suna?" His indifference to the cult was my only remaining reservation.

"Yes," he replied firmly. "Tell me more about them when we

get back. I've been thinking about what you said. I didn't know." I felt the words vibrate in his chest.

"They're terrible. And not just because of... the goddess. You have to do something."

"When we get back, I will. If they still insist on having Eros-suna, they should be a places of joy and... mmm... pleasure." He nuzzled my head. His heart beat a heavy rhythm. His intoxicating body, so in tune with mine, called to me, but this wasn't the place. Other people—other *gods*—could appear at any moment.

"Could we get away from here until tomorrow?" I whispered. The ceremony didn't sound real to me yet, but the danger from Cytherea did.

He looked down at me with a grin. "Yes."

❧ 29 ❧

EROS

No cloak. No bindings. Just my wings spread wide on the wind. My back flexed almost painfully as I clutched Psyche to my chest. I hadn't exercised my wings in years and the added weight meant more flapping, more stamina. And *fuck*, it felt good.

Psyche winced and held tighter as I angled down, streamlining my body to dive through a gap between mountains. Far below was the God-King's palace, nestled among the peaks. It looked huge even from the air.

Up here were clouds and wind and rocky heights. And there was freedom.

I laughed as we dove, Psyche's hummingbird heart fluttering against my own. Catching an updraft, I leveled us out again. From here the ocean came into view, sparkling on the horizon. Its splendor stole my breath and stirred my longing for home.

"Oh!" Psyche's cry barely rose above the roar of wind. She'd seen it too.

All my worries fell to nothing. Fear and betrayals belonged down there, not here with me and my lovely, lethal bride. Together we'd make a way.

REALITY DIDN'T SETTLE UNTIL THE NEXT DAY. SINCE WE'D stolen away from the palace, I couldn't keep an eye on Lox. Cytherea might have tried talking him out of nominating us. She certainly had powers of persuasion.

Hand in hand, Psyche and I paced down the wide halls of Thenios' palace. Others walked past us, sometimes within arm's length. I fought not to flinch. I'd decided to be brave, to not give a fuck what anyone thought. But years of ingrained terror didn't just disappear all at once.

Familiar ideas barreled back.

What if Psyche betrays you again?

What if Cytherea sent another assassin to kill you here before the ceremony?

What if Psyche is killed instead?

That last one gripped my mind in a fist. Psyche didn't have wings or height or strength. She had will.

When I pulled her closer, she gave me a questioning look. We hadn't learned each other yet. Not really. But now we'd have forever. In the past, that would have been the thought that scared me. Bound to one partner for eternity? It would have sounded more confining than the bonds I placed on Psyche before the wedding... or on our wedding night. But now the commitment didn't frighten me much. Psyche was surprising and sexy and a little terrifying. She was wild. I liked wild.

Sunlight through the windows grew dimmer. The eclipse was coming.

We hurried into the Ascension Chamber. It lay at the heart of the palace, built around a sacred spring. Nine massive thrones, all empty, stood in a raised semi-circle facing the spring, which bubbled from a circular opening flush with the floor. Water lapped gently over the stone lip. Across the spring from the thrones was a rectangular altar. Above everything loomed a large skylight surrounded by detailed constellation charts.

A few smaller chairs on the side held dignitaries, priestesses, and assistants. I headed there.

Psyche, still all in gold like a liquid statue, gaped at the enormous room. Maybe she was thinking what I was—that this was really happening.

We stole a look as we sat side by side. I hadn't seen her this nervous since I'd woken to find her brandishing a knife over my bed. Her temperature rose several degrees.

"The God-King Thenios!" declared a naked announcer by the door. The young man looked as if he'd been dipped in gold himself.

Thenios emerged from a grand set of double doors. Above his bearded chin, his eyes flashed lightning. The toga he wore looked like the royal version of mine, though he had no practical reason to choose an antique one-shouldered outfit. He sauntered, barefoot, to the center throne. Immediately, two attendants, also nude, offered him grapes and wine. He smiled indulgently at them.

"Cytherea!"

I scowled as the goddess entered next, trailing a fond finger along the announcer's jaw as she passed. Psyche stiffened beside me. Her heart beat so fiercely, I couldn't focus. I squeezed her hand.

"Basileus!"

I'd never seen the god of the ocean before. Thenios' brother had much darker skin and a stronger physique, obvious because he wore no shirt. He had a deep rent in the skin over one eye. His outfit was a tailored set of sleek brown trousers and iridescent green mantle that matched the faint scales glittering on his strong cheekbones.

"Ares and Bellona!"

The back of my neck prickled. The conflict between the War Twins had threatened my seaside palace multiple times, since it faced their Realm. They didn't acknowledge each other as they stalked like predators into the room. I only recognized one. Ares had short-cropped hair and a smear of red across his eyes. He visited my mother regularly in the past. Although my mother never confirmed it, I always suspected Ares was my father. I ground my teeth. In the palace on Mount Venut, he'd called me weak, soft, emotional. He'd mocked everything about me except my proficiency with archery. I'd forgotten he would be here.

Bellona, his sister, had lighter skin and matching black makeup barring her face. She wore her dark hair shaved on the sides. Weapons bristled out of the leather outfits they wore.

Prowling to opposite ends of the room, they settled in the thrones farthest from each other.

That explained why there were nine thrones instead of eight.

"Lox!"

I perked up. Lox glowed faintly as he entered. The eclipse was deepening, casting the room in shadow, which only emphasized his otherworldly shine. The crown on his curly head reminded me of sun rays. He dressed in a stylish white suit. I tried to catch his eye as he made his way, smiling faintly, to one of the thrones. He didn't acknowledge me. My stomach knotted.

Attention locked on the others, I didn't even see Vesta come in.

Scira—more conspicuous because of her piercings and rattling hair ornaments—brought me back to the moment.

"Hades!"

The other gods watched the door warily after the final name was announced. Hades ruled the Far Realm with all its punishments and mysteries. I'd never even seen a map that showed the whole island. Normally, just the southeastern tip jutted into view. In every way, his reputation was wreathed in secrets and menace.

We all took a few breaths, waiting, before Hades himself stepped in to watch our ascension ceremony. I felt gooseflesh rise on Psyche's skin. I ran a finger over the back of hand, but I felt the chill too. Hades' eyes were distant, assessing. His hair was jet black, darker even than Psyche's, but the skin under his trimmed beard stubble was pale. His clothes were neat, simple, and expensive. The god of the dead didn't smile or acknowledge the others as he took his place.

When I glanced at Psyche, she stared at the line of rulers, awestruck and a little defiant. I could have licked that look off her face. It gave me courage.

"Do we have candidates?" King Thenios asked, almost carelessly.

My attention darted again to Lox, one of the favorites. *Say something.*

Bellona's war-sharpened gaze sliced to me and Psyche, as if the answer were obvious. Her focus through the black warpaint unnerved me.

Cytherea, on the other hand, refused to look at us. Despite how aloof she acted, I felt every particle of her attention.

Irena, graceful, seemingly materialized beside Lox's throne. She whispered into his ear. Did he not even know to vouch for us? Dull anger simmered inside me. I'd demanded sacrifices like some god of ancient times, suffering isolation that strung every nerve so tight it threatened to snap, and Psyche had almost killed me, all in pursuit of the freedom godhood would provide... and he didn't know? My throat constricted as Lox gave Irena a smile, casting his light on her before she stepped back into the shadows.

"Yes," he said, finally glancing at me. "I believe we have two."

"Do they have your nomination to ascend?" Thenios asked from his center throne.

"Yes."

"Their names?"

"Eros and..." He looked at me as if I needed to supply him

with Psyche's name. Irritation welled up next to my anger. He should know her name. They should all know her name.

I opened my mouth to answer.

"Psyche." The voice belonged to Scira. She hissed the name as if it were an incantation, her ornamented hair clacking.

"Psyche," Lox repeated, as though he'd known it all along.

I had no idea how Scira knew Psyche's name. Her reputation was mystical, the realm of mind and spirit, but I didn't know practically what that meant. Could she read minds? It didn't matter right now. At least someone knew who Psyche was.

I slipped my hand from hers to caress her waist, drawing her closer. Her body, solid and warm against my side, grounded me. The anger that would have built and built under strapped-down wings and a heavy cloak dissipated next to her.

"Eros and Psyche," King Thenios repeated grandly. He considered the deathless to his right and left. "Do they have our blessing to ascend?"

Psyche's heart tripped. I felt not only her blood pulse faster through her veins, but Cytherea's as well.

"They obviously have mine," Lox reaffirmed. I was starting to get the sense that he was more of a little shit than a magnanimous deity, but I still owed him massive gratitude for nominating us, so I bit my tongue.

"It is for the best," said Scira in that inscrutable, unsettling way of hers.

Cytherea finally scoffed.

I knew it.

"To ascend to godhood is a tremendous responsibility," she began, "and one that is eternal. Do you want to immortalize the demi-god of *lust*? He cannot be trusted. Lust and passion are chaotic, fleeting things."

"With no strategic plans for overthrow," Bellona, the goddess of war, cut in sharply.

"Accidental destruction is still destruction," Cytherea replied smoothly.

Next to her, Bellona's brother Ares offered her a poisonous smile of agreement. I knew I hated him.

"I have no plans to destroy," I said, "and I've married a mortal to prove I am no threat to the Realms. I don't want power. I only want freedom. For me and Psyche."

The gods stared at me. Suddenly, I was vulnerable, killable, a bug in sight of a frog. I forced air in and out of my lungs. In and out. The only person here more vulnerable than me was Psyche.

She stared at me too. I latched onto that look, those eyes. A line formed between her brows, fear mixed with determination. I could drown there, in that look, in that connection, in that woman who knew the dark of my paranoia and the light of whatever bravery I'd managed to claw back.

"Psyche." The voice was Cytherea's. "The girl who served *my* temple."

When I finally acknowledged her, she regarded Psyche with motherly compassion. I seethed.

"Don't you want rest instead of strife?" Cytherea asked her. "Not long ago, you said you hated Eros. An eternity with him won't fulfill you." She opened her arms. "You've done well. Years of faithful service at my temple have earned you a place at my side. Come with me to find pleasure and rest, away from all this."

I knew what Mother was doing. Without Psyche, I wouldn't ascend. Lox nominated us together. If Psyche gave into this offer, I would die, if not by her hand, then by a broken heart. I had no idea how I was so tethered to Psyche after this short time. She'd tried to kill me. We'd both lied and refused to reveal parts of ourselves. But I was smitten and didn't see myself untangling my affection enough to get free. My little wife was fierce and bold and kind and beautiful. I needed her.

As she listened to Cytherea, Psyche's eyes shone glossy. She panted as though she were enduring torture. I rubbed her waist gently, reassuringly. If she chose to go back to the goddess she served all her life, I wouldn't stop her.

Freedom wasn't freedom from death or fear. Freedom was knowing Psyche would be safe and happy, whether I was there to witness it or not.

30

PSYCHE

"*You've done well.*"

I *hurt* when Cytherea said those words. Before, she wouldn't acknowledge that she knew me.

So which was the lie?

I'd longed to hear those exact words for so long that I couldn't remember the first time I worked for the goddess's approval. Her temple had given me shelter when I had none. Her strong figure had adorned my daydreams for years. I wanted to be her. But now...

What did I want now?

I did want the peace she offered. I did want pleasure. I just didn't want it in her service anymore. Eros showed me that I didn't have to sacrifice myself to be loved.

Tenderness softened the goddess's eyes as she looked at me. Me. Psyche. I swallowed a hard lump in my throat.

"I don't think you mean that," I managed.

Next to me, Eros exhaled.

"Of course I do," Cytherea continued. "You've completed

as much service as a god could ask of a mortal. I'd be happy to call you one of my own."

"I thought I was one of your own before."

"You've been faithful your whole life. I'm offering the reward you crave."

My pulse rushed like the ocean in my ears. All the ruling gods were watching us, but I couldn't revere Cytherea the way I did before. I couldn't. "I want to ascend with Eros," I said, my voice growing stronger.

"No, you don't." Her gaze flashed, although her tone stayed seductively sweet.

"I do."

"I will not allow a murderer to ascend." All her empty praise poofed into nothing. She addressed the other deathless gods. "Will you?"

My chest felt leaden and my head weightless. My secret was coming out now? A sort of joyful despair took me. Whatever my fate, at least it would be based on truth.

Yes, I was a murderer.

I loved Eros.

And I disavowed my goddess Cytherea.

"A murderer?" King Thenios repeated, attention sharpening.

In the following pause, I didn't deny it. I searched at the faces of the other gods. No one seemed as surprised as King Thenios, which gave small comfort.

"Yes," Cytherea replied. "For her service, I would grant her sanctuary, but I cannot allow this abomination to take place."

"Is this true?" This time, Lox asked the question.

I couldn't help meeting Eros' eyes before answering, "Yes. I killed a man outside the temple when he attacked me, and... and I killed another man several years ago for the same reason." My eyes stung. So many years keeping the truth hidden, only for it to come out like this...

"She was attacked," Eros said loudly. "I forgive her. Why can't you?"

My skin flushed. Why would he of all people forgive me? My willingness to hurt others wasn't a surprise to him, but wouldn't my admission make him think twice about allowing me to ascend?

He flashed defiance at Cytherea, who sat immovable as a mountain. I felt his muscles tense. Maybe he expected her to lash out.

"Did you 'forgive her' for attempting to kill you, too?" Cytherea purred.

I set my jaw, glaring. How much could we say in front of all these gods? Thenios stared with obvious interest, but no criticism. Hades looked bored. Ares, amused. No one seemed as if they'd strike out at us. No one but Cytherea, that was.

Finally, Eros turned back to me. The muscles in his throat flexed. Such an interplay of soft and hard, strong and fragile, shone in his eyes. Pain glowed in that look. This was it, the moment I became too much and not enough. The moment he would leave me.

His magnificent wings formed a backdrop to his concerned expression. That effortlessly sensual mouth, that tendency toward forgiveness that bordered on naïve, that desire to learn and love... My chin trembled. He was right. I wasn't enough for him. "I'm sorry," I whispered, forcing myself to nod. "It's okay."

There was no need to point fingers at the goddess. We both knew—maybe the whole group knew—who had pointed me at Eros like a weapon. But I had agreed to do it, so it was still my fault.

He grasped my hands in his. "I do forgive her," he said, answering the goddess's question but not taking his eyes off me. "And I'm sorry for everything too," he whispered.

I sank my teeth into my lower lip to keep it from quavering. His gaze followed the gesture.

Eros knew my worst parts, that I had murdered twice before, but he didn't leave me. Even if our lives weren't deathless, this moment made everything worth it. Lox's glow lit one side of Eros's pale golden face. Time stretched.

"Does anyone else object to this ascension?" Thenios asked.

"Me."

My head snapped up to see who had spoken. Ares, god of war, who sat next to Cytherea. My heart dropped.

How many gods did we need to complete the ceremony? Cytherea wanted to kill Eros, and I had just refused the goddess's offer. If we didn't get permission to ascend now, we'd both be dead within the year. I tried to steel myself, to stand up straight, to be proud of the woman I'd become, capable of standing up to the deathless. In the face of these beautiful, fearful gods and their judgment, though, it was difficult.

"Please," sneered Bellona, Ares' sister. The nearby kingdom of Eriset suffered constant war because of these two fighting. Refugees sometimes tried to flee for sanctuary in Aphriso. "How will one horny god harm you or your plans?"

Plenty of stories came to mind, but I said nothing.

When Ares didn't respond with anything but a withering grin, Thenios repeated his question. No one else objected. "Six of eight agree?" he asked.

All bowed their heads in assent.

"That's enough," Thenios declared. "Do they have the sacrifice?"

Eros didn't respond. Instead, his eyes grew wild. *Did we not have a sacrifice?*

Thick silence blanketed the darkening room.

"It must be a death-sacrifice," Lox explained.

My skin froze, lips numbing in terror. I'd heard of animal, and even human, sacrifices in the distant past, but most cultures didn't do that anymore, I thought. Did the gods still demand blood?

From her throne, Cytherea smiled.

A warm chuckle came from Thenios. "You make it sound so dire for your candidates, Lox. Few choose to sacrifice a bull or a child like the old days."

My blood curdled.

"A little death will do."

Did I hear that right?

Hades sighed, exasperated.

I started shaking with silent laughter. The absurdity and coincidence of it, the nerves, everything, almost made it impossible for me to stop.

"We choose a little death," Eros answered. I nodded.

"Do you require assistance?" Thenios asked, his eyes a little too keen as he ran his knuckles down one of the naked servants beside him.

"No." Eros cheated a look at me. "Each other."

I smiled, still laughing. It was as though I'd been training for this my whole life. Looking up at the arranged gods, though, tension writhed in my gut.

"You are *each other's* sacrifice? Hmm." Thenios hummed to himself, obviously pleased. "Then you must sacrifice at the same time, with each other, and strike simultaneously."

Strike simultaneously? As in, orgasm at the same time? In front of all the ruling gods? A helpless smile crossed my lips. If anyone could do it, Eros and I could, though I'd rather take him almost anywhere else. His wry expression mirrored mine. He was ready to do it too.

Thenios addressed a priestess about the appropriate constellations for us, but at that point, I was barely listening.

The room was so dark that Lox began to draw every eye. In his glow, I noticed the war goddess tightening her hold on one of the knives in her leather outfit.

Despite his light skin, Hades seemed to fade into the darkness. One less person to watch me and Eros have sex on the altar. At least, it sounded like that's what they were talking about. I had no qualms about having sex in public, but in front of every god-ruler of the Eight Realms?

Just being in their presence left me breathless. These were names I'd heard my whole life but never expected to see. Not only had I met Cytherea, the goddess I spent my life serving, but I'd seen every other, all beautiful and terrifying in their power.

With the eclipse gaining strength, the reality of the ceremony hit me low in the gut. This ceremony would make me a goddess. An actual goddess.

If I could time my little death with Eros's. I couldn't wish for a better partner for that task.

Talk of constellations done, another priestess approached the water in the center of the room—probably a sacred spring —and told us to rise. I stood stiffly beside my husband. After our flight yesterday afternoon, I still felt sore from clenching my muscles, but the glorious experience was worth every ache.

I saw an echo of Belaria in the priestess's face when she handed us a bowl of water, and something in me hardened. Eros reached for the bowl but I got to it first. He glanced at me in surprise.

"Drink," the priestess said smoothly.

I did, and then handed the water to Eros.

This time, I wouldn't be cast out. This time, I wouldn't be abandoned or dismissed.

I'd be a goddess, the same as Cytherea.

A piece of me felt inadequate for that honor—the piece that reared its head whenever I looked at the nine thrones— but the rest wanted to shove it in her face. I was ready.

That ritual done, voices chanted our names in conjunction with our stars. The sun barely eked out light. Shapes dimmed in the Ascension Chamber.

"The eclipse is nearly total," King Thenios announced. "Your sacrifice will complete the ceremony." A lecherous smile lifted one side of his mouth as he gestured to the altar.

So I was right.

It was stone, not very comfortable, and well in sight of the whole audience. If we only had minutes, maybe I couldn't finish this last part.

As if reading my mind, Eros stepped in front of me,

blocking the others from view. He cupped my face. "Just focus on me."

I stared at his sensual mouth and deep-set eyes, but desire had left me. A rise of panic wiggled its way into my heart. My mouth went dry.

"Focus on me," he repeated, then, lower, in my ear. "I'll get you there."

Normally, that was my job. An offering of pleasure to the goddess meant helping others experience release, even when I didn't reach it myself. Now the role was reversed.

"But we have to come together," I whispered back.

"When you think you're close, lift up on the base of my wings like you did that night. Just don't pretend."

I could tell he was aroused from the gravel in his voice. Good. I just had to trust him. Which wasn't the easiest thing with the literal pressure of eternal life bearing down on me.

"Shhh," he soothed, kissing my cheek.

The eclipse was almost at the full.

Eros laid me down on the stone altar before crawling on top of me. He truly was beautiful. Every move he made begged for another body to move with him, over him, under him. I tried to relax. But the stone was hard and all the gods stared at us.

With a wicked smirk, he smoothed up my golden dress until it came off. Gripping the dress in one hand, he took off his own robe. I got a good view of his perfect body, all the muscles rippling down to his erection, already half-hard. He was so big. If I wasn't ready to take him in, the pain would stop me from coming too.

Gold. Gold covered my face, cool as silk. The cloth tightened as Eros tied the dress over my eyes.

A blindfold.

"You're with me. Here. Feel my body adoring yours." Eros breathed hot against my ear. He raised my arm and licked the crook of my elbow as he rolled his hips, teasing my entrance.

I relaxed a little.

He lowered himself to kiss me on the lips, hungry and wanton. His hair mixed with mine against my face, and I answered, sucking his soft bottom lip into my mouth. He tasted like salt and sugar, like sin.

I gasped as his fingers found my crease and kneaded the same way I'd shown him in his bedroom. I never thought he'd imitate me. My spine peeled away from the hard stone surface. Finally, felt myself go wet. That aching pulse started to pound. Maybe we could do this after all.

"Stay with me," he murmured. He smelled like musk and sky. His movements grew more insistent too.

I gripped his upper arms and hit the golden cuff. His fingers changed their rhythm to something—gods, something I liked even more. I whimpered.

"Yes?"

Then he slung my legs over his shoulders. I cried out as he buried his face between them.

In front of all these gods...?

Oh, but the sensation was so delicious that I writhed even as he gripped my ass to keep me in place. He hummed, the vibrations turning me molten. I grabbed the sides of the altar to keep myself from squirming off. He knew I liked this, how rare this was for me.

And I was need. A void.

"Now," I huffed.

He parted my legs to get them off his shoulders. My ass hit the stone, but he held my knees up as he pressed himself inside.

Farther, farther...

I was surprised every time. He went so deep I felt him everywhere. He made a filthy noise as he pushed in his full length. His thrusts were insistent, just hard enough not to hurt. It was that firm pace I liked. Shit, he paid attention. Once he knew *everything* I liked, I'd be drunk on him for weeks. Maybe for eternity.

"Ah!" I breathed. "Gods, yes!"

The place he rubbed with his cock craved release but the pleasure and need only built higher. Higher. Higher...

I scrambled for his wings, hooking my fingers around and pulling up on them with all my might.

Eros felt like a taut string ready to break. I couldn't see him, but his tension turned to trembling. Was that enough time for him?

He pumped into me one, two, three more times. My whole body contracted. I couldn't hold on. I arched high, shaking as the little death took me under. In the wave of release, I heard a frantic groan, sensed Eros pull out, felt lines of cum crisscross my torso.

A loud clap made me jump. "Oh!" Thenios exclaimed with a throaty laugh. "And precisely at the height of the eclipse. You were right about these two, Lox."

I yanked off my blindfold, blinking in the hazy light. Eros panted on top of me. He'd managed to help me forget the watchers long enough to orgasm with him. Even as unfamiliar embarrassment scuttled over my skin at the thought of Thenios and Hades himself watching me, I was proud of us. We'd done it. If Cytherea had brought a shield, it would have reflected true pleasure instead of its counterfeit.

Eros and I stared in wonder. The ceremony was over.

Then I gasped, my whole body suddenly on fire. Pain, pain everywhere. Inside me, where I couldn't reach. I twisted as my vision turned white. Eros' strong hand held me down. He asked me what was wrong. I didn't know. I couldn't answer.

All I knew was fire.

31

EROS

"What's happening to her?" I demanded, jumping off the altar.

"She's becoming a goddess," Thenios replied evenly.

I stayed protectively near Psyche as she convulsed. A scream ripped from her mouth.

"What does that mean?" I yelled furiously.

"Not many humans become gods," Lox said. The words came out careless.

Beside him, Cytherea watched Psyche writhe, unmoved.

I could hardly hear Lox above the shredding sound of my love's agonized cries. My heavy breathing after we'd successfully reached our death-sacrifice together had transformed into panic.

Something moved under her skin.

"I'm here," I said, ignoring the others now. "I'm here, love."

The room was dark, eclipse full, but a sliver of light let me watch the pain etched in Psyche's every feature. What had I done? I'd allowed this, all for my own godsdamned safety. What was safety if the ones I loved had to suffer for it?

"Help her!" I whirled on the rulers, still sitting on their thrones as if my bride weren't thrashing in pain on the altar.

Thenios shrugged. *Shrugged.*

I gritted my teeth. My thoughts didn't often run to violence, but if I didn't hate the thought of leaving Psyche's side, I would have flown to the God-King and punched him in the mouth.

Why weren't they concerned? Had Cytherea managed to harm her at the last second?

The shrieking ceased. My attention snapped back to Psyche. She lay motionless, head lolled to one side. She looked stretched out, exhausted and empty. Her body didn't look the same, though I couldn't pinpoint exactly what had changed.

I placed one hand over the hot skin above her heart. It beat a fast, steady rhythm. Her chest rose and fell. Evidence of our quick orgasm still glistened on her.

"Psyche," I rasped, nestling closer to speak in her ear. "Psyche. Can you hear me?"

Her lips parted and eyelashes fluttered as she squinted up at the darkened ceiling.

I released a sob. "Psyche." When she groaned, I held her tenderly against my chest, lifting her up from the stone slab.

"You didn't think that the amusing aspects of the ceremony would be enough to make you ascend, did you?" came Hades' voice from where he lounged elegantly in the shadows.

I did my best to ignore him. My eyes were wet and Psyche's body was warm and alive. She felt different, and I finally figured out what had changed. She had grown. She was taller, no longer tiny. I ran my hand along the full length of her back. The bones of her spine protruded as if in protest against what had just happened.

"We did it," I said against her hair. "Will you be all right?"

She struggled before answering, "I think so."

As I held Psyche in my arms, I stole a look at Cytherea, who glowered back.

A priestess appeared beside us, bringing more spring water, this time in an ancient-looking vessel. It was aged bronze, inlaid with faded gold designs and black gems. "Eros and Psyche," she murmured, as magical as Scira was. She pressed the cup into my hands. I gave it to Psyche.

The priestess prostrated herself before us with a low, chanted prayer to the divine.

With shaking fingers, Psyche set down the golden dress, still clutched in her fist, and brought the cup to her lips. Her sweaty face revealed how much effort even that simple movement took. I drank next, matching my lips to where hers had been. Bronze made the liquid taste like blood.

The sliver of light from the waning eclipse grew brighter.

All the attendants bowed to us. Only the ruling gods themselves didn't kneel.

"Eros and Psyche," Thenios repeated in his booming voice. "God of passion and goddess of spirit."

Only Cytherea didn't echo the words back to him. She couldn't kill me anymore. I held Psyche closer. I had my bride, and I was free.

"You did wonderfully," I whispered, combing my fingers through Psyche's tangled hair. She winced at my touch. "Hold your breath, love." Without waiting to be dismissed, I stepped through the air back to my seaside palace in Aphriso.

Psyche grunted in pain as we arrived in the home I hadn't visited in almost fifty years. My bedroom had barely changed. The aroma of tropical foliage surrounded us, fragrant and alive. Statues I'd commissioned them for parties stood on pedestals. They depicted couples and groups in positions of sensuous rapture. My bed took up nearly half the large room, low and deep with blankets. Unlike the crumbling fortress in the mountains, this castle had light walls with delicate carvings and luxurious amenities. Here, with Psyche, my skin seemed to fit again. I flapped my wings.

As I disappeared, I'd grabbed the gold dress. Setting Psyche gently on the bed, I began to ease it back on her. She breathed deeply, leaning her forehead against my chest as I worked the fabric over her arms and down her sides. As I finished, I knelt to look at her eye to eye, letting my hand linger on her thigh. Tired, she met my gaze.

"Are you all right, love?"

She nodded sleepily.

I patted her gently, my chest full to bursting. "We did it."

"Where are we?" she asked, squinting.

"A safe place." I couldn't keep the grin from my face. "Home."

Her eyes lit up. "Is this...?"

I nodded.

She pressed a kiss to my lips. With a sigh, I crawled up on the bed, curling my body around hers. She was definitely taller than before, fitting against my entire front. After the stone altar, my bed, even smelling faintly of mold, felt heavenly. I'd replace the blankets soon.

"You stood up for me." Psyche's quiet voice reached a deep place within me.

"Of course." I kissed the back of her head. "You chose me over Cytherea."

I felt rather than saw her smile. "Every time."

"Should we... Do you still want to talk about the Eros-suna? I do, but... maybe not right now," I admitted, nuzzling into her hair.

"Later," she said, lacing her fingers through mine.

I draped a wing over us, protective. "Later. Right now, I have a goddess in my bed."

She squirmed against me, pleased and obviously feeling better. Something in my core loosened. I hated seeing her in pain.

"You know," I said low in her ear, "I'd like to see many people adore you. This bed is big enough."

Her heartrate kicked up and temperature soared.

"Yes?" I coaxed, pleased she didn't find the idea foreign or repulsive. She had been a temple courtesan, after all. Imagining the scene—glorious Psyche surrounded by others dedicated to her pleasure while I drove into her, at least on one side—made me harden again. The thought of so many bodies gave me a momentary check, but I could dismiss it now that Cytherea couldn't murder us. Ever. If Psyche wanted an orgy, nothing was stopping us.

"Not just me," she said, caressing the top of my hand with her thumb. "Us." She twisted until she faced me. The movement made her grimace, but this time the discomfort was short-lived. She reached around me, holding me, softly stroking my wings. I soaked up every touch. Then, her dark eyes went glossy. "I'm glad I get eternity with you," she said, voice breaking.

I swallowed, blinking away my own emotion. How lonely had these years been? How many times had I thought I'd never find someone I could trust, who would love me in return? Psyche was everything I wanted. More home to me than this long-abandoned palace. "I love you, Psyche."

She kissed me, soft and firm. "I love you too, Eros."

EPILOGUE: PSYCHE

I caught my own reflection on the shield hanging on the wall beside the arrows and quiver. Sweaty, happy, messy, flushed. Eros probably positioned me in that direction on purpose. He liked to watch the pleasure on my face.

I never pretended anymore. Whether I felt pleasure or not, I was truthful. That way he could continue to know me, to learn me.

And *gods* had he learned me.

I pitched forward in ecstasy as he spread me wider, drove deeper, teased my waist with the feathers of his contracted wings. His thrusts were sure yet searching. He always searched for new way to please me, a new pitch of intensity for me to fall apart. He made me feel known, as if each part of me was infinitely precious.

Around us, others coupled too, rhythmical, gasping, almost a dance.

Utterly different than the temple.

I saw nothing but the soft, cream-colored blanket in my

clutched fists. My ache grew, pulsing hard and insistent as a desperate itch, but Eros wouldn't satisfy it. He waited, teasing, rubbing, coaxing out every last bit of maddening desire. No wonder I was on my knees.

He leaned close, one wing brushing the underside of my breast. "My favorite place," he huffed in my ear, "is your skin. The hot slick of your pussy on my cock. It's when you let me kiss the sole of your foot. Psyche." His voice hitched.

I gritted my teeth. I couldn't take much more.

Maybe the others could sense that their god and goddess were close, because the chorus of grunts and cries pitched louder.

"Yes, yes," Eros hissed, all hot breath. "That's it. Fuck!" He pulsed into me as his orgasm rocked him hard. Shuddering and deflated, he pulled out. Expert fingers filled that empty place, rubbing just the way I needed, firm, with friction.

I couldn't speak, just rode his fingers until the blanket disappeared behind closed eyelids, my mouth opened, and inarticulate sounds came out as waves of relief exploded around my clenched thighs.

Out of breath, I opened my eyes and reality returned. I eased myself up from the bed, turned my back to the shield, and faced my husband, the greatest lover I'd ever known. His eyes were soft with drunken desire. Slowly, he traced the inside of my thigh, where I'd gotten a tiny butterfly tattoo to represent my freedom.

With a smirk, I ran my hand up his leg to where he'd gotten one in the same place, except his was a bow and arrow, a new variation of the popular design in Card.

As the others finished, collapsing onto the bed, Eros raised an eyebrow at me to indicate one couple. Would they make a good match for each other?

I watched them for a moment. They touched each other with fierce care, checking in with unspoken questions. Their interactions reminded me a little of Eros and myself.

I nodded back. Eros gave a lazy smile. He had a knack for matchmaking. By the time humans and demi-gods found themselves at one of our celebrations, though, there was usually little to arrange. No encounter could be one-sided or go further than everyone wanted. Before wine was brought out and the bed laid with pillows and oils, everyone agreed on terms.

Today's terms included lavishing me with praise and attention. Before Eros took me all to himself, others caressed me, ground against me... It was heavenly. And rightly so. We were celebrating.

All the cult groups disbanded after Eros visited them himself. I went with him. With my added height, everything felt smaller, as if I had grown into the temple statue myself. Now that we were both deathless gods, he ordered two temples to be built near the small seaside province of Silkuoma that we ruled together. One would be the only official Eros-suna. The other, a Psyche-suna, although the term still set me laughing with how absurd it sounded.

"Their goddess of spirit," he had murmured against my skin the night after construction began.

Every spring and fall, Eros would oversee a celebration in his temple. I'd oversee mine every summer and winter.

With the building projects underway and the dissolution of the corrupt Eros-suna, it was time for a party.

This was the second day of the revel, and I was enjoying it immensely.

After a wash, a feast waited for us outside our room. Servants, excited by the notion of Eros returned (his replacement Agafya hadn't ruled with the same generous abandon Eros did), set out roast fish and lemon, bread with herb butter, poached pears, sour rolls filled with sheep cheese, crab, grain and leaf salad, and white wine. I beamed at the incredible spread. Eros caught me looking and gave a private smile. His eyes shone with tender adoration, warmer than anything at the feast.

"Lord Eros."

He tore his attention from me to the servant who had addressed him.

"Two people at the gate."

"What do they want?"

"The male says it's the ninth day of reckoning."

That sounded vaguely familiar, but I couldn't place the strange saying. Eros, on the other hand, grew rod straight. A tinge of panic touched his features. No, not panic, but something with edges just as sharp.

"What is it?" I asked.

In answer, he took my hand and strode toward through the breezy inner courtyard to meet the visitors himself. It didn't take long to reach entrance and, beyond that, the gate.

Behind it stood Zepherin and Cressida.

I gasped.

"Passwords?" Eros began, angrier than I would have expected. His feathers bristled. I knew from all our late-night talks how deeply Zepherin's betrayal still stung.

Zepherin scanned the length of me, something dawning in his expression. Cressida's wide, defiant eyes took in Eros—she'd never seen him until now—before she turned to me.

I flung open the gate and collided with her in a hug before I knew what I was doing. I stood taller than she did now. "Why didn't you tell me you were leaving?" I hissed in her ear. "You know I wouldn't have told."

Over Cressida's shoulder, I caught Zepherin and Eros sharing a look that thawed some of the ice between them.

"I couldn't," she replied, her voice muffled against my shoulder. "I didn't know what would happen. I didn't know it was Eros. He could have been a monster." She dropped her voice. "He was a little monstrous, what he did."

"A lot monstrous," I agreed.

Cressida released me with a concerned question in her gaze, but I simply smiled. It wasn't difficult to smile anymore.

"I heard what happened during the eclipse," Zepherin said, his tone softer, less sure. "I wanted to congratulate you."

Eros pursed his lips. "Did you?"

I touched his forearm lightly.

Zepherin's expression was open, ready for whatever forgiveness or punishment we'd hand down. He linked hands with Cressida, united.

Eros sighed. He tucked me against his side in a comfortable motion. "I always wondered when you'd fancy someone," he told Zepherin. "I thought you and Olitor would make a good match."

I gasped. "The gardener?"

Zepherin laughed, a foreign sound. I liked it. It started in his chest and burst out in uncontrollable little chuckles, as if he'd been taught to hold it in.

Eros smirked and nodded his head in the direction of the mountain. "He's still tending the plants up here. You and Cressida... I know you have memories there, but that old fortress is yours if you want it. Psyche and I like it here better."

What a perfect idea! Zepherin and Cressida didn't need to live on the run. They could have a castle of their own. I suspected that Cressida would do better things with it than Eros had when he feared for his life. Relief washed over Zepherin's features at the pronouncement. The couple gave each other cautious grins.

"Monster of the mountain," Eros quipped, before releasing me to draw Zepherin in for an embrace.

The soldier looked utterly flabbergasted at the contact.

I laughed and grinned. The way Eros faltered when he turned his attention back to me made my insides plummet. That look could dominate me. I couldn't get used to catching a god romantically off guard.

"Yeah, monster of the mountain," Zepherin agreed breathlessly. The thought seemed to please even Cressida.

Eros drew his arm around my waist again. "You've earned at least that for putting up with me all these years."

Zepherin gave a curt nod of thanks. I couldn't help remembering what he had witnessed here on the steps to the palace. Thankfully, his penance was over.

"We do," Cressida agreed. She acted almost disappointed that there wasn't going to be a fight or argument to win.

"Come inside. We're about to eat," I urged. What was the use of having so much if I couldn't share it with more friends?

As we four headed into the palace together, Eros said to Zepherin in a low voice, "There's a person here that I think would be perfect for Olitor. Tell me what you think."

Smiling, Cressida and I rolled our eyes.

I liked this playful side of Eros, this free side. We were all free, I reasoned. The bonds that held us tight before had disintegrated. It was a new world.

I looked up at Eros, smiling easily with his friend, and thanked the gods I got to taste this new world with him by my side. The god of sex and the goddess of spirit. What could be better?

THANK YOU!

Thank you for reading *Wings and Blindness*! Please consider leaving a review. Reviews help authors like me get found by more readers.

Now, read on for a sneak peek of a Hades and Persephone inspired story that will leave you begging for more...

Once upon a time...

No. Fuck that. My life was never a fairy tale. A long time ago when there were fewer gods and a savage cluster of islands, my brother declared himself the all-powerful ruler and divvied up the land among us. I was never his favorite, never saw him as the true mastermind behind the Great Victory that left us in charge, so he sent me to the Far Realm. It was barely close enough to be called part of the Eight Realms, but I figured he liked it that way. His God-King status could reach farther. Besides, he never admitted to fearing me, but he saw what I did in the war, so I had my suspicions.

I manned the deathless prison—not an easy task—and set up my own kingdom. The Far Realm, it turned out, was enormous. I never told anyone. In fact, I actively thwarted any attempts to chart it unless my own cartographers did it. *I* had to know what was there. No one else had to learn about the silver and jewel mines, or the winter forests, or anything else about my property. They knew I was wealthy and dangerous. That worked for me.

And the Far Realm was dangerous. After being unceremoniously ousted to the far reaches of my brother's territory, I found... not a soft spot, but more a direction for my spite in accepting all the rejected demi-gods and creatures. The malformed and terrifying.

Even the dead.

The war in Eriset gave me too much opportunity to make good on that offer. For the price of two coins, I'd accept human corpses if they were sent across the sea to me. Most of them still had their spirits attached. I did what I could to give them an afterlife. No one was so thoroughly rejected than the dead. There wasn't enough manpower to help them all, but I did what I could.

With the war heating up, corpses arrived every day. My workers couldn't keep up with demand. Some of the spirits themselves helped me, an ever-growing business of souls, but I could see them wearing down every time a spirit disconnected before we could glean it. Even my considerable resources stretched to the breaking point trying to deal with this problem, and it wasn't going to let up soon.

I hated asking for help. Hated it. And no one offered, which worked for me. I preferred to be left alone to rule my kingdom the way I wanted. But now I needed someone else who could capture the human spirits or even reanimate the bodies that were still intact.

I exhausted myself trying to manage the whole load—the dead, the prison, the unpredictable demi-gods. Even taming myself was an ongoing task. Now, finally, I had to do something about it.

Sitting on my throne beside the eight other rulers—yes, eight (Ares and Bellona constantly fought for control of Eriset) —I crossed my ankles. I'd only come to this godsforsaken eclipse gathering because I was out of options. Unfortunately, though, that meant I had to sit through inane meetings and distasteful ascension ceremonies. The chamber grew dark as the planets cast the sun in shadow.

Lox, that golden boy, literally glowed beside the God-King, casting the only light. If he hadn't nominated two beings—a demi-god and a human—for ascension to godhood, this meeting could have adjourned and I could finally ask the only question on my mind: Were any new abilities discovered in the census?

But that would have to wait. Below us, a priestess offered water to the couple Lox had nominated. It came from the sacred spring that had conferred godhood to all of us, probably, at one time. I didn't remember. More than one human spirit asked where I had come from. What a stupid question... Nobody remembered their own birth.

I dimly recognized the demi-god. Eros, Cytherea's son. He had massive white wings. A much smaller human girl stood beside him. After they both drank, they headed to the altar for a death-sacrifice. Evidently, Eros had forgotten he needed to bring one. That was fine with me. I didn't like to see more bloodshed than I had to. People assumed I liked death, being the god of death and all, and I didn't correct anyone.

I drummed my fingers on the armrest of the throne as the two disrobed and got on the rectangular altar by the spring. Glancing up at the skylight, pale constellations painted like outward-facing fractures in the marble, I quirked my lips to the side. At least this wouldn't take long. Either they'd find their little death by the end of the eclipse or they wouldn't and they'd have to try next time. In ten years. If they survived.

I didn't have particularly high hopes. It was an unforgiving world.

The worst thing about this display was my brother Thenios' obvious enjoyment of it. A glance showed me that he didn't miss how well hung Eros was. Thenios even leaned forward a little as Eros thrust his face between the girl's thighs.

I tried not to pay so much attention. I'd seen a hundred of these ceremonies. I hadn't come here to gawk at a pretty couple. I had serious business to attend to. Most of the others seemed to regard these meetings every decade as an opportunity to party and socialize. Half the time, I didn't come at all. Too bad for the nominees for godhood in those years. Honestly, I could do without any more beings who were truly deathless.

Thrusting against each other now, the panting couple emitted whimpered cries. Eros' white wings contracted around them, sheltering the woman from view. I shot another glance at my brother, whose interest hadn't abated.

Annoyingly, the crotch of my tailored trousers bulged with arousal. I ground my teeth. *Just breathe through it.*

Deep within, I sensed a claw running along the inside of my belly. A question. The answer was no. Glowering, I held myself at bay.

A life of celibacy wasn't what I would have chosen for myself, but it was for the best. Unlike my siblings, I couldn't simply bed someone and move on. Many reasons. My obsessive side came out at inconvenient moments, I had no time, and perhaps most importantly, I respected my subjects enough not to expose them to my unpredictable darkness unless their conduct warranted punishment. My subjects respected me and I wanted to respect them. No one else had. Weighed on a scale, the health of my kingdom mattered more than a good fuck. Even if I sometimes really, *really* wanted a good fuck. It had taken years to leash the creature within, to make him obey. I wouldn't undo all that because I wanted sex. Denying myself didn't improve my mood, but it did make my efficiency knife sharp. My high-risk population needed every ounce of my attention.

Besides, no one wanted to live in the "horrible" Far Realm with monsters and an emotionally unavailable partner with... dark tendencies.

The couple on the altar reached a fever pitch. Reluctantly, I found myself watching them. They were sensual together, playing each other like instruments. It helped that they were both undeniably gorgeous. She writhed. He thrusted. Then, her head snapped back, mouth open. In Lox's glow, sweat gleamed on her neck. With a loud grunt, Eros peaked too, finishing with a frantically pumping hand along the hard length of his cock.

I let out a sigh, subtly adjusting my position on the throne. At least that was over.

Now onto business.

READ *FLOWERS AND THE FAR REALM* NOW!

READ MORE BY ZORA FOX

Fae and Shadow duology
End of the Forest
Trapped by the Fae

Deathless Love series
Wings and Blindness
Flowers and the Far Realm coming soon!

Find all of Zora Fox's spicy fantasy romance titles on Amazon.